Sugar Spinelli's
Little Instruction Book

People who say money can't buy you love just don't shop hard enough. That's what I told Twyla McCabe when we first heard about the Lost Springs Bachelor Auction. Over the years, she's learned to listen to me, and I'm proud to call myself the first and most loyal client of Twyla's Tease 'n' Tweeze Salon.

You know what beauty salons are like. We talk about everything there. And I mean everything. Which means mostly men. We love 'em, we hate 'em, we can't live without 'em. This Rob Carter, though. Would have picked him out myself, but he and Twyla are made for each other. She just doesn't know it...yet.

Dear Reader,

We just knew you wouldn't want to miss the news event that has all of Wyoming abuzz! There's a herd of eligible bachelors on their way to Lightning Creek—and they're all for sale!

Cowboy, park ranger, rancher, P.I.—they all grew up at Lost Springs Ranch, and every one of these mavericks has his price, so long as the money's going to help keep Lost Springs afloat.

The auction is about to begin! Young and old, every woman in the state wants in on the action, so pony up some cash and join the fun. The man of your dreams might just be up for grabs!

Marsha Zinberg
Editorial Coordinator, HEART OF THE WEST

HUSBAND FOR HIRE
Susan
Wiggs

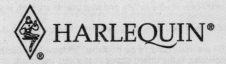

HARLEQUIN®

TORONTO • NEW YORK • LONDON
AMSTERDAM • PARIS • SYDNEY • HAMBURG
STOCKHOLM • ATHENS • TOKYO • MILAN • MADRID
PRAGUE • WARSAW • BUDAPEST • AUCKLAND

Susan Wiggs is acknowledged as the author of this work.

ISBN 0-373-82585-4

HUSBAND FOR HIRE

Copyright © 1999 by Harlequin Books S.A.

Visit us at www.romance.net

Printed in U.S.A.

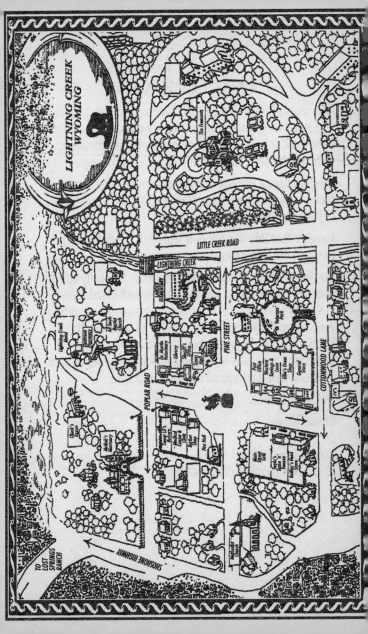

A Note from the Author

As a resident of a remote island in Puget Sound, I consider myself a very experienced catalog shopper. I thought I'd seen it all, from sheer lingerie to burpless cucumbers, until the Bachelor Auction catalog came into being.

Imagine paging through a glossy brochure filled with pictures of gorgeous men offering to take you on any date of your choosing.

Imagine that this was not only legal, but politically correct, because the funds went to a good cause.

No red-blooded woman could resist this. Certainly not I! I happily jumped right into the fantasy, and found myself in the very heart of the West, writing a story filled with laughter and tears and just a little bit of matchmaking. I hope you'll join Twyla and her loyal salon customers in Lightning Creek, where all bachelors are eligible, all days are good-hair days and all dreams come true.

Warmest wishes,

Susan Wiggs
Box 4469
Rolling Bay WA 98061-0469
http://www.poboxes.com/SusanWiggs

To the real Sugar and Theda,
who are even more fun in real life

Acknowledgments

Thanks to fellow writers Barb, Betty, Christina and Joyce, for reading, critiquing, listening and egging me on. Also thanks to Sister K and Sister B for giving this a thumbs-up.

Thanks to the Wyoming State Visitors Bureau, especially to Karen in Casper for answering (with a straight face) all my most off-the-wall questions. Technical expertise was generously supplied by Dr. Paul Reims. Technical expertise and big hair were also provided by the Fluff 'n' Stuff salon in Poulsbo, Washington.

A very special, heartfelt thank-you to my editor, Marsha Zinberg, who conceived this project, launched it with her usual creative flair, listened to the wackiest of ideas and made working on it so special and rewarding.

CHAPTER ONE

"HONEY, YOU NEED A MAN," said Mrs. Duckworth.

"A what?"

"You know, a man. A large male human being with big shoulders and no neck."

Twyla McCabe picked up a rat-tail comb and expertly squared off a lock of Theda Duckworth's silvery hair. "I once had one of those and he did me no good at all. I have a dog."

Mrs. Duckworth gestured at the other customers in the salon. "The girls and I have been discussing the issue, dear. It's time you found yourself a man." She spoke with exaggerated patience.

Twyla leaned forward over the vinyl swivel chair and checked Mrs. Duckworth's roots. "Sweetie, I think you've been pickling in Number Four lavender dye too long. Why would I want that kind of trouble?"

Mrs. Duckworth caught her glance in the large round salon mirror. Twyla's baffled gaze was no match for the no-nonsense glare of a retired third-grade teacher.

"To take you to your high school ten-year reunion," Mrs. Duckworth said.

Twyla plunked the comb in a stainless-steel tub of Clear-Glo solution. "Diep," she said, turning to her manicurist. "I told you not to say anything about the reunion. I've already made up my mind."

Diep Tran didn't look up from painting Mrs. Spinelli's nails. "I never say a word."

"But you showed everyone the invitation, right?" Twyla asked, feeling her face turn hot and hard with embarrassment.

"I show everyone a picture of you wearing a crown," Diep said unapologetically. She bent her head over her customer's hand, using a minuscule paintbrush to illustrate a little slice of watermelon on each nail. When it came to painting theme nails, Diep Tran had no peer. She was the Georgia O'Keeffe of nail art, fulfilling all requests from anatomically correct Greek gods to the words Divorce Me! in block letters. Her presence in the salon had increased business and kept a steady stream of nail customers coming back on a regular basis. But she had a problem minding her own business.

Twyla was still amazed the Hell Creek High School reunion committee had found her. After everything that had happened, she hadn't told anyone in her hometown where she had gone. But somehow, the reunion invitation had found its way across Wyoming to her.

"How often do we get to see you wearing a crown, hon?" Mrs. Duckworth asked, chuckling. From beneath her smock—a pink one with the salon's sequined ruby slippers logo on the pocket—she extracted the Reunions, Inc. newsletter. The front cover featured a picture of Hell Creek High School and a photo montage of students from ten years before.

Lord, had they ever been that young? Twyla wondered, her gaze drawn to the layout. The smiles of the graduates burst with self-confidence. The bodies were young and strong, the attitudes positive. A tangible glow of limitless possibilities seemed to emanate from each youthful face.

Life hadn't happened to those kids yet. Every one of them believed utterly that the world was theirs for the taking.

The largest picture, in the center, showed a much younger Twyla, with sparkling tiara, on the arm of a young man who looked at her with adoring eyes and an expression that gave no hint of what was to come in the years that followed that moment.

Twyla was almost ashamed of how vividly she recalled that night, when she seemed to know exactly how her life would turn out, when her dreams soared higher and farther than the confines of the little western Wyoming town where she was born and raised.

So much for the girl most likely to succeed.

Diep and Sugar Spinelli held an earnest, whispered conference at the nail station. Mrs. Spinelli's earrings flashed, but not so brightly as her eyes.

Sadie Kittredge lifted the hair dryer from her pincurl set and took the invitation from Mrs. Duckworth. "Who knew?" she asked, her bemused gaze flicking from the photo to Twyla. "You were Cinderella."

Twyla snatched the invitation away. "Uh-huh. And look how she ended up."

"She lived happily ever after. Everyone knows that."

Twyla tapped a box of foil squares against the palm of her hand. "So how come we never read about what came after, hmm?"

"Kids, mortgage, in-laws…who wants to know?" Sadie winked and popped her gum. "So you're going, right?"

"No," Twyla said. "Do you know where Hell Creek, Wyoming is?" Agitated, she took a square of foil and busied herself wrapping Mrs. Duckworth's hair, section by section.

"Of course I do," Mrs. Duckworth said, indignant. "I was a teacher for thirty-five years."

"I'm a lowly school psychologist," Sadie admitted. "You'll have to give me a hint."

"It's a gazillion miles from nowhere," Twyla said. She finished with Mrs. Duckworth and peeled off her plastic gloves. "Almost to Jackson. It's certainly not close enough for me to drop in just to say 'hey' and have a beer. Even if I could afford to be away from here for a weekend, I wouldn't waste my time at a high school reunion."

"Oh, sweetie, it wouldn't be a waste." Sadie handed her an issue of *Woman's Day*. "Says right here that keeping in touch with old friends is good for your mental health."

"It also says the way to a man's heart is through his stomach," Twyla pointed out, putting down the magazine. "I think that's aiming too high."

"Sure thing you don't like men," Diep observed with a soulful shake of her head. "They are not all like your first husband."

Twyla tried not to think about Jake, but each time she did, she saw him in her mind's eye, proudly holding his law degree. In a moment of pure faith and hope in the future, she had married him straight out of high school. He had been in his third year of college, a lavishly handsome man full of heady ambition. How could she have guessed her plans would unravel so swiftly and brutally, that she would flee her hometown in shame and grief? Since then she had discovered there were worse things than being dumped by a man you thought you knew.

"You mean my *only* husband," she stated. "I'm not interested in a second one."

"You just haven't found the right man," Sugar Spinelli said. Thanks to a husband who pampered her outrageously, she spoke with a feminine knowing that was hard to argue with. Petite, white-haired and smiling, she had the serene look of a woman who had known the love of a good man.

"I'm not looking," Twyla said, seating Sadie in the next chair for her comb-out. "I don't run into many in my line of work." She gestured around the salon with its cotton-candy-pink appointments.

For the past three years, she'd been sole proprietress of Twyla's Tease 'n' Tweeze. She had read in a book somewhere that a place of business should have a corporate identity, a recognizable symbol. Twyla had chosen the ruby slippers from *The Wizard of Oz*. Red-spangled shoes adorned the clock, the sign out on Main Street, the smocks, the framed prints on the walls. Twyla herself wore red clogs to work every day, and Diep had adopted the habit, as well. The ruby slippers always reminded Twyla that all the magic she needed was inside her.

Except that Twyla's magic was pretty darned unreliable, judging by the swiftness with which the bills stacked up in the salon and at home. She didn't mind. She substituted hard work for New Age concepts. "And it's not like I can go to the market and just pick one out," she added.

"As a matter of fact—" with a bob of her foil-covered head, Mrs. Duckworth took something else out from beneath her smock "— you can."

"What's that?"

The older lady exchanged an infuriatingly coy glance with Mrs. Spinelli. "Oh, something mighty special. Sugar and I have been talking about it for days." She hugged a glossy catalog to her ample chest. "I guess you all are familiar with Lost Springs Ranch."

Twyla nodded, mildly intrigued. Everyone knew about the foster-care facility located off the Shoshone Highway. The ranch had a decades-old reputation for taking in boys who were homeless, orphaned, in trouble or labeled incorrigible by their families or society.

Sometimes the ranch was the last stop before reform school or prison, and thanks to an intensive program, Lost Springs got a shot at turning a troubled boy's life around. Twyla suspected that the success rate was due, at least in part, to teachers like Mrs. Duckworth.

"Well, I'm sorry to say they're running a little short on money," she continued. "But they've come up with one crackerjack of a fund-raiser."

"Wait till you hear," Mrs. Spinelli said, holding out her hand to inspect her nails. Afternoon sunlight streaming through the plate-glass shop window glittered off a not-so-small fortune in rings and bracelets. She and her husband owned thousands of oil-rich acres, and she had become driven and relentless in her philanthropy. "It's a fabulous idea. Tell them, Ducky."

Mrs. Duckworth held out the catalog. "A bachelor auction."

Twyla rolled her eyes and started unpinning Sadie. "I've heard of those things. Crazed and desperate women bidding on men who think they're God's gift. Sounds silly to me."

"So take a look at this, Miss I-got-no-use-for-a-man. It's easier than picking out burpless cucumbers from a seed catalog."

"Oh, for heaven's sake, let's see that." Sadie grabbed the brochure. Her freshly tweezed eyebrows shot up. Her mouth formed a perfect *O* of surprise. "For heaven's sake," she said again, only this time her tone was quite different.

"All right, we look together." Diep snatched the catalog and spread it out on the pink Formica counter. She was so short that Twyla could stand behind her and still see over her head—and what she saw extracted a snort of laughter from her.

"What is this, Frederick of Hollywood?" she asked. "Who are these guys?"

"The men of your dreams," Mrs. Duckworth declared. "Each of them lived at the boys ranch at one time. They're the fund-raiser."

"Bimbos. Boy toys." Twyla turned up her nose. "They're all alike."

"Uh-uh," Sadie objected. "They all have different faces, see? We have to have some way of telling them apart."

"Honestly," Mrs. Duckworth blustered. "This is reverse sexism at its worst. I simply don't understand you young people."

"What they selling?" Diep demanded, her gaze locked on a studio photo of a dangerous-looking guy on a Harley.

"Themselves, hon." Mrs. Duckworth studied Diep's face. "I don't guess you've ever heard of a bachelor auction."

"Livestock auction, yes," Diep said. "My father once bought a Nubian goat at auction. But bachelors? These men?"

"Uh-huh," Twyla said. "You bid on them, like Nubian goats."

A look of wonderment suffused Diep's pretty, doll-like face. "And then what do you do with them?"

"I reckon you do anything you want." Sadie Kittredge flipped the pages, perusing a cop, a park ranger, a businessman, a golfer, a cowboy…and caught her breath. "So long as it's legal."

"She's right," said Mrs. Duckworth. "The gal who outbids all the others gets a date of her choosing. All the money goes to the ranch, and some of the bachelors have voluteered to match the funds." Her foil wrap clanked as she turned to Twyla. "So have a look, and tell us which one it'll be."

She laughed, half amused, half incredulous. "Pardon me?"

"Which guy?" Sadie said with an excess of patience. "You're going to pick one out to escort you to your high school reunion."

"Uh-huh. And then I'll click my heels together and wind up in Kansas."

"Really, Twyla. It's too perfect," Mrs. Spinelli said, warming to the idea. Her grape-size amethyst earrings bobbed in rhythm with her excitement. "We all agree you need a man, you want to make a big impression at your reunion—what better way than to show up with the perfect fantasy man?"

"Wait a minute. I've been trying to tell you—I don't need a man and I'm not going to the reunion."

"Yes, you do, and yes, you are." Mrs. Duckworth injected thirty-five years of stern third-grade teaching experience into the statement.

For the sake of keeping the peace, Twyla changed tack. "Even if I was interested, I don't have the money. I'm a single mom, my business runs on a shoestring, and the last thing I can afford is to plunk down my hard-earned money for some spoiled..." She made the mistake of glancing down at the rancher in the leather vest and chaps. "Overprivileged..." Her gaze wandered to the next page, where a man in an Armani tux, holding a long-stemmed red rose, smiled up at her. "Narcissistic..." The next photo showed a man in a chef's apron and cap, and apparently nothing else.

Exasperated with her wayward imagination, she forced her attention to Sadie's comb-out, taking great care as she unwound her best friend's honey-colored hair from the pins. "Anyway, I don't have the money or the inclination, so let's just drop the idea, shall we?"

Passing her hand lovingly over the glossy pages, Mrs. Duckworth emitted a long-suffering sigh that immediately squeezed Twyla's conscience. It was for a good cause, after all. And despite her protests, the idea of a bachelor auction was shamefully tantalizing. Suppose a man materialized out of thin air, like a genie from a bottle, to be her date for just one night? Then she'd have something to show off at her class reunion, something besides a life that hadn't turned out anything like the life she'd envisioned ten years ago.

"Look," Twyla said, "these guys are out of my league. They're looking to raise thousands of dollars from each bidder."

"Out of *your* league, maybe," Mrs. Spinelli said, drumming her freshly painted nails on the counter.

Twyla raised a hand in protest. "Oh, no, you don't. I'm not letting you spend your money on a date for me."

Mrs. Spinelli laughed. "Last year I paid two and a half grand for the prize pig at the state livestock show. And that poor creature wound up at the slaughterhouse."

"A bachelor would be a lot more fun," Sadie pointed out. "And you wouldn't feel sorry for him when it was all over."

"Absolutely not," Twyla insisted.

Four long faces fixed her with stony, accusatory stares.

She squirmed, trying to think of a distraction. "Maybe we could go along to watch the festivities. We'll bring that quilt my mother's finishing for the county hospital society. We could raffle it off at Lost Springs and make a group donation to the cause."

"You're no fun," Diep grumbled. She pointed to the

short bios that accompanied each photo. "You read us this, yes?"

"Here's a good one." Mrs. Duckworth stopped at the half-naked chef. "Age—thirty-something. Job—investment banker and aspiring kitchen god." She rattled off the rest of the bio, and it was all nauseatingly predictable: star sign, biggest achievement, favorite song, car. Most embarrassing moment. "Oh, poor man, he was making chicken cordon bleu for a date and it burned up when they got carried away and forgot to turn the oven off."

Sadie ran a caressing hand over the smiling hunk. "You know, I read in a magazine article that hunger and passion create the same expression on a man's face."

Mrs. Spinelli shook her head. "You mean all these years I could have just fed Roy?"

Giggling, Twyla kept reading. "Oh, perfect. It says here his ideal woman has long blond hair and is free-spirited. Translation—he's looking for Malibu Barbie."

"What's that?" asked Diep.

"Hot sex with no commitments."

"All right, so that one doesn't work for you." Mrs. Duckworth doggedly took her through a few more bios. Each one would have the reader believe that a woman's looks weren't important to him, that he was a sensitive guy under the rugged exterior, that he drove a Porsche 911 because it was "practical," that his intentions were honorable, his career path straight as an arrow and his sense of humor boundless.

"You know," Twyla said, "before we start drooling too much, we ought to remember where these guys came from."

"The Lost Springs Ranch for Boys," Mrs. Duckworth said. "That's why they volunteered to be auctioned off."

"They were juvenile delinquents. Some of them were

abandoned or orphaned as children." Twyla thought of her own young son, Brian, and a soft rush of sympathy spread through her. "It's bound to leave scars." She pointed to the bull rider, whose ice-blue eyes hinted at a world of secrets within. "You have to wonder what sort of baggage they're carrying around inside them."

"I bet he'd show you if you asked nicely," Sadie said. "God, that mouth. Think he's related to Val Kilmer?"

"I think it's a perfect marvel that they've all grown into such successful, upstanding men," Mrs. Spinelli said.

"Single men. You have to wonder," Twyla said. "If they're so wonderful, why aren't they married?"

"You don't always find your heart's desire the first time around," Sadie observed with a wise nod of her head.

Twyla numbed herself against a twinge of hurt. Sadie didn't mean anything by it. Not too many people in Lightning Creek knew much about her past, but Sadie, her best friend, had a pretty good idea of what Twyla used to dream of and what she had given up when her marriage had ended.

"That's true," she said. "But you know, I've got something better here. I run my own business and have the world's cutest kid. When I was younger, I had no idea how important those things would turn out to be." Still, she sometimes lay awake at night, haunted by the feeling that she had settled for less than her dreams. "I'll be the first to admit that I blew it with my first marriage. The thing is, I don't want a second time around. I like my life fine as it is."

"But wouldn't it be a little more fun if you'd date every once in a while?" Sadie, who dated more than once in a while, was always pushing Twyla to get out more.

"Oh, look," said Mrs. Duckworth, paging through the catalog. "It's little Robbie Carter." She pointed to the rose-and-tux guy.

"Not so little anymore," Diep said.

"I remember him from my third-grade class. My, my, he did clean up nicely, didn't he?"

"He's a doctor," said Mrs. Spinelli.

"And a Leo—that's a good sign," Sadie added.

Twyla brushed and spritzed her hair, listening with only half an ear. He spoke Spanish, loved to travel and drove a Lincoln Navigator. He was the chief partner in a Denver pathology lab. She found herself vaguely disappointed in the thumbnail bio in the catalog. The guy was so extravagantly good-looking, so accomplished, she almost hoped to find something in his story to set him apart from the others, something in his tragic past, perhaps, that told her a man of character was buried beneath that polished exterior.

"Says here he put himself through school on a sports scholarship and hard physical labor. Wonder what sort of labor," Mrs. Spinelli said.

In spite of herself, Twyla perked up at that. Imagine, a man who actually took responsibility for his education—if that was what he'd really done. She supposed, when a guy was out to sell himself, he'd say anything. But she lost interest when Mrs. Duckworth announced Carter's ideal woman: an educated city girl with a high-powered, socially responsible career. Translation: Malibu Barbie with a degree and a pedigree.

He should stay in the city, then, she reflected with a small shake of her head.

One by one, they went through the bachelor auction brochure, giggling, sighing, arguing the merits of a single earring versus a row of studs, and whether a park ranger or a toy manufacturer was better at satisfying a woman.

"Are you kidding?" Sadie said with a laugh. "What kind of toys do you think the guy makes?"

Twyla put the finishing touches on her hair. "There. You're Jennifer Aniston."

Sadie eyed herself critically in the mirror, tilting her head this way and that, then holding up a hand mirror to view the back. Her butterscotch-colored hair fell like silk over her shoulders. "Oh, hon, you outdid yourself." She went to get her checkbook.

"So which one would it be?" Mrs. Duckworth asked playfully. "Just for fun. Out of all of these guys, which would you pick?"

Twyla knew they would hound her until she answered. Just for fun, then. "All right," she said, perusing the glossy pages while her heart beat a little too fast. "Um, let me have another look at the narcissistic doctor."

CHAPTER TWO

"I CAN'T BELIEVE I LET you talk me into this." Rob Carter scowled at the sage-covered hills speeding past as he drove the black Explorer he'd rented at Casper's airport. Although nineteen years had passed since he'd traveled this road, he remembered every oxbow curve, every hill and every valley on the way to Lost Springs Ranch. Remembered the shimmer of heat rising off the asphalt road and the occasional busy oil well, the rig pumping like a big metal crow jabbing at seeds. Most of all he remembered his relief at leaving the small-town life of Lightning Creek.

Static crackled over the wire of the car phone. Then Lauren DeVane's silky laughter flowed through the speakers of the car. "Darling, I can't believe you're so reluctant. It's all in fun, and Lindsay Duncan is one of my dearest friends in the world. When she asked for help raising funds for Lost Springs, I didn't hesitate a nano-second."

A flicker of movement caught Rob's eye, and he braked, slowing the vehicle. A pronghorn leaped across the road and disappeared into the sage-and-ochre-colored wilderness. A white tail flashed, then the animal disappeared down the far side of a hill. "Yeah," he said to Lauren, "but you're not the one who has to get auctioned off like beef on the hoof."

"But I'm the one who has to stand by while another

woman buys a date with you.'' He knew a smile had softened her voice. Lauren was gorgeous, brilliant, and way too sure of herself to feel truly threatened by the prospect.

"Then you bid on me," Rob said, scanning the roadside for more pronghorns. "That would solve everything."

"I can't reschedule this trip to San Francisco. Besides, that would violate the spirit of the entire event. The appeal of two strangers meeting is a powerful fantasy."

"Not mine." Rob eyed the rushing white line down the middle of the highway, his nerves tensing tighter with each mile. "Maybe you should come and find a cowboy of your own."

She laughed again, her cultured voice filling the car, making him smile. "What is this romance people have with ranch life, anyway? Cowboys are obnoxious and socially impaired. I need that urban polish, Robert. Besides, I've had this trip to the Bay Area planned for ages. I can't possibly get away." She paused. "I'll miss you, though. I'll be thinking of you every minute."

"Ditto." Rob wondered if she understood how relieved he was that she wouldn't be at the auction after all. Born and bred into a life of unimaginable wealth and privilege, Lauren had no clue what his childhood had been like. He'd just as soon keep things that way. He wanted to protect her from the knowledge, because she had a heart that bled at the slightest hint of tragedy.

She never asked him about the past, about what it had been like growing up at Lost Springs Ranch for Boys. It wasn't that she didn't care. The truth was, she didn't want to know. She didn't want to see that, despite the spit-shine of his hard-won success, he would always be a man with no family, no pedigree, no name except the one scrawled on a form by the mother who had abandoned him.

He pounded the steering wheel, mad at himself for feeling the slightest breath of self-pity. Lauren had a heart as big as the West. It wasn't her fault she could never understand the way he had grown up. And it wasn't his job to explain it to her.

"I'd better ring off now, darling," she said. "I have a hair appointment. I'm getting it cut."

"Shorter?" he said, disappointed as he envisioned her glistening waterfall of hair as it spilled across his pillow—one of his favorite sights in the world.

"No, silly, longer." Her easy laughter drifted across the miles. "Of course shorter. You'll love it."

"Whatever." People who cut off a woman's beautiful hair should be shot.

"Bye, darling. Call me tonight."

Rob turned on the radio to fill the silent void after the phone call. A twangy voice wailed out, "Don't come knocking at my door unless you can deliver the goods...." He passed a road sign that read Lightning Creek 1 Mile, and despite the sunbaked heat of the day, he felt a chill inside. He hadn't been back here since he'd walked away at age seventeen and hitchhiked to Casper, where he caught the train east. That day, he had vowed never to come back. There was nothing here for him, nothing but a sleepy western town and a lot of wild countryside.

But when the plea had come from Lindsay Duncan and ranch director Rex Trowbridge, Lauren hadn't allowed him to ignore it. The place was in trouble and in danger of closing. All the ranch alumni were being asked to help. Rob had volunteered to write a generous check, but Rex and Lindsay wanted him there in person, and in the end, he couldn't refuse them.

His life had been saved, literally, by Lost Springs. If his mother hadn't taken him there at age six, she probably would have left him in some run-down motel room, forgotten like an old shirt hanging on the back of the door. He didn't remember much about his mother, but he did recall that she tended to forget things.

Like the fact that she had a son waiting for her in Wyoming.

He took the exit for Lightning Creek, slowed his speed as he approached the town limits, then turned onto Main Street to have a look around. A place apart in time, Lightning Creek had barely changed. The storefronts of Main Street retained an Old West character of weathered wood and hand-painted signs, a railed boardwalk and the occasional rack of antlers affixed over a doorway.

Memories jostled into Rob's consciousness. He remembered saving up money for a cheeseburger and chocolate malt at the lunch counter the locals had dubbed the Roadkill Grill. Less pleasantly, but more vividly, he recalled being caught shoplifting at the General Store. Across the street was an establishment he didn't remember from the past—a beauty salon called Twyla's Tease 'n' Tweeze, complete with bubblegum-pink facade and red shoes on the sign.

A waste of space, he thought. Who needed a place where women paid good money to get their hair all cut off? He shuddered to think of the local yokels who went there.

Looking ahead, he rounded the traffic circle with its statue of a cowboy on a bucking bronc. Eternally frozen with his arm flung up, the statue was a town symbol and landmark. A lot of the boys of Lost Springs had dreamed of becoming cowboys and winning rodeo competitions, maybe even owning their own spread one day.

Not Rob Carter. To him, the wildness of the country called to a place inside him he didn't like, and the small town felt clannish and claustrophobic. With the same dogged determination many of the boys had given to working with the livestock at the ranch, Rob had pursued his studies. Math, science, physics. They gave him a sense of order and logic, led him along a path to a career that depended on precision and judgment. His single-mindedness had been fueled by ambition and, in the tiniest possible measure, fear.

He had exacted from himself the highest test scores, the best grades, the most unforgiving schedule, because that was his means of escape. The grueling tasks he set for himself were conquered, one by one, like boulders surmounted by a rock climber. College, completed on a full scholarship and supplemented by horrific hours working as an orderly. Medical school, internship, residency. Now, a full partner in a lucrative medical lab in Denver, he had earned a small fortune.

And damn, it felt good.

Crossing Poplar Road, he headed north and pulled into the parking lot of the Starlite Motel. Like the rest of the town, the place had changed very little. It had a neon sign with a star eternally blinking and the Vacancy sign perpetually turned on—except for the letter *n*. Feeling doubly glad that Lauren hadn't come here with him, Rob checked into his room.

The room had a lumpy bed, but the linens were fresh and clean. The single window framed a view of the pool, an aqua-tinted lozenge in the middle of the cracked parking lot. Rob set down his bag and wished the vending machine outside carried beer. He could use a cold one.

Later, maybe. Tonight there was some sort of get-together for the guys involved in the auction. He wasn't sure how he felt about that. He knew a few of them but they were a part of his past, and he had done more thinking about the past today than he had in years.

He took a few minutes to unpack his belongings. Lauren had been his chief adviser in this, suggesting what to wear in order to fetch the highest price. Stuff with designer labels, stuff you saw on members-only golf courses. She had dressed him for the photo shoot for the brochure, putting him in his custom-tailored tux. He hated his tux, but it drove Lauren wild. And knowing Lauren, she was probably right. You look the part, you're worth the bucks.

Going to the window, he watched a young mother cross the parking lot, pushing a stroller with a fringed sunshade. Two older kids raced ahead, making a beeline for the motel pool. A bright beach ball spun through the air. Shrieking, the kids went after it while the mother took the baby on her lap and rubbed sunscreen on its chubby arms and legs.

Against his will, Rob felt a surge of…something. Just for a second, he thought it was yearning, but he quickly buried the notion. It was probably something he ate.

CHAPTER THREE

"Okay, sport, are you about ready?" Twyla called, glancing at the clock over the kitchen stove.

"Coming!" With a drumroll of running steps, Brian raced downstairs. He never walked anywhere. To his mind, if a place was worth going to, it was worth running to.

Twyla met him in the foyer just as he grasped the banister and his feet left the floor, swinging out and around the newel post. "Brian, I told you not to—"

"Oops," he said as the knob came off in his hand. With a sheepish look, he handed it to her. "Sorry, Mom."

"Fifteen minutes early to bed tonight," she said. To a six-year-old, it was an eternity.

"Aw, Mom—"

"You have to learn to take it easy on this poor old house."

"Yes, ma'am."

As she fitted the wooden peg back into the hole, she felt an unwelcome glimmer of the resignation that always seemed to be lurking at the edges of her life. Built in the twenties, the house sat on a knoll a little north of town. It had a big yard and a tree with a rope swing and that peculiar weary charm of an old, long-lived-in home. But it also had the liabilities that came with an old house—inadequate wiring, leaky plumbing and a variety of wooden aches and pains.

That was the only reason Twyla had been able to buy the place when she'd come to Lightning Creek, pregnant and shell-shocked by events back in her hometown. The property had been remarkably affordable. It was a little more challenging to pay for its upkeep.

Chastened, Brian was subdued for about ten seconds. Head down, freckled face solemn, he looked—momentarily—like a kid on a greeting card illustration. Twyla wasn't fooled. She knew the next bit of mischief was never far away. Reaching out, she smoothed his sandy red hair, smiling when the cowlicks went their own way. "How's that loose tooth of yours?"

He tilted back his head and wiggled it with his tongue as he spoke. "Thtill looth."

"I think it's ready to come out," she suggested. "Want me to pull it out for you?"

"No way!" He clapped his hand over his mouth.

She smiled; it was the one thing he was squeamish about. "All right. Carry that box of raffle tickets, would you, sport?" she asked.

"Sure, Mom." Picking it up, he raced out to the pickup and jumped in the passenger side. She could see him bouncing up and down on the seat, and his exuberance made her smile. With just two weeks of school to go, he could hardly bear to wait for summer vacation.

"Are you sure you don't want to come with us, Mama?" Twyla called. Her mother was in the small suite of rooms off the kitchen, an add-on from the forties. Twyla's invitation was automatic. So was her knowledge of what the reply would be.

"No, thank you, dear," Gwen said, coming into the foyer. As always, she looked scrubbed and spry. Her

Bermuda shorts and cotton shirtwaist were spotless, her cropped hair pure white and beautifully styled.

Somehow, her mother's attractiveness made things all the more frustrating and baffling. A widow for the past seven years, Gwen lived with her daughter and grandson, watching Brian while Twyla worked. At first it had seemed an ideal arrangement, every working mother's dream. It was a luxury to have a loving grandmother in the house, baking and singing and reading stories. Now Twyla looked back on those starting-anew years and wondered if there was anything she could have done to prevent Gwen from developing the affliction that had shadowed them for so many years.

If Gwen had any clue to her daughter's thoughts, she gave no sign. "I was browsing through that bachelor brochure you brought home from the shop."

"See anything you like?" Twyla asked, teasing.

"Oh, heavenly days, not for me. I was thinking of you, dear. You might as well go for one of the younger men. They never mature, anyway."

"Mother, really—"

"They're all a bit young for me." Her eyes, which looked so blue in contrast to her white hair, glinted with mischief.

"Depends on what you buy them for," Twyla pointed out.

Gwen eyed the crooked newel post. "Maybe if you get one cheap, you could bring him home and get him to work on the house."

Twyla laughed. "I didn't see any home-improvement specialists in that brochure."

"Not knowing how to fix something never stops a man from trying," Gwen pointed out.

"True. But I'm not buying. Just going along to sell

raffle tickets for the hospital guild quilt.'' She patted her mother's hand. ''You did a gorgeous job on it, Mama.''

''It was a pleasure to work on.'' The Converse County Quilt Quorum met once a week at Twyla's house, twelve ladies stitching and gossiping over the long afternoon. Their creations had become local legends, coveted for the freshness and energy of their designs. Twyla always wondered at the way a basket of mismatched scraps and snippets could be magically transformed into a work of art.

She got her keys and went out to the truck as her mother waved through the front bay window. The rusty '74 Chevy Apache wasn't pretty, but the pickup was too reliable—especially in winter—to send to the junkyard. Just for fun, Twyla had applied a magnetic Tease 'n' Tweeze sign to the door. The pink sign, with its sparkling ruby slippers logo, looked incongruous against the gray undercoat of the truck door she couldn't afford to have repainted.

As she took off, she glanced in the rearview mirror. The geraniums in the window boxes were blooming, but one of the second-story shutters hung crooked. The contrast between the beautiful flowers and the run-down house was not funky; it was simply pathetic. Maybe she should get a small apartment in town where she wouldn't have to worry about upkeep on a big place. Then she thought of Brian, racing with Shep across the yard or climbing the rope-swing tree, and she dismissed the idea. She wanted her son to be raised in a family home, even if the family consisted of only a mismatched and troubled mother-and-daughter set.

As they approached Lost Springs, Brian sat forward, his narrow chest straining against the seat belt as he stared out the window. His tongue worried the loose tooth.

"So what do you think, sport?" she asked. "This is a nice place, isn't it?"

"I guess." A split-rail fence lined one side of the road. In the distance, a herd of horses grazed placidly through tufts of mint-green meadow grass that grew in the shade of a clump of oak trees. Dust dervishes swirled across the sun-yellowed pastures. Summer had come early to Wyoming this year, and on the slope behind the main building, wildflowers bloomed, a snowfall of avalanche lilies, goldenrod, Indian paintbrush, purple heliotrope and long green fronds of high grass.

"This is where Sammy Crowe lives," Brian said with a reverent hush in his voice. "The boys who live here are orphans."

"Some of them are, yes." Twyla didn't know a lot about the ranch, though it had been a fixture in the area for many years. Sammy, the boy in Brian's class, rode the bus in to school every day. One of the first-grade mothers had whispered that the boy's mother was doing time in the state women's detention unit. "Some of them are here because their parents can't take care of them."

"Like my dad couldn't take care of us?"

Twyla forced herself to stare straight ahead, keeping her face expressionless. With Jake, it hadn't been a case of "couldn't" but "wouldn't," though she'd never tell Brian that. "Not exactly," she said carefully. "You have Grammy and me to take care of you."

"But who takes care of you and Grammy?"

She glanced sideways. "We take care of ourselves, kiddo. And we're doing all right."

"All right's good enough for us, Mom."

She grinned, turning her gaze back to the road. It was

hard to believe how quickly Brian was growing and changing. How wise he seemed sometimes, for his age. She wondered if that old-soul streak of maturity came from being raised without a father. Some nights she lay awake, racked by doubt. She was raising a wonderful boy, but she couldn't help worrying that there were things a father could give him that a mother and grandmother could not. They were the intangibles. That unique chemistry that existed between dads and kids. She'd felt that magic with her own father. He'd had his faults, but his love had enriched her life beyond compare. How would she have turned out without it?

She worried sometimes that Brian would always be missing a small, settled corner of his heart that should be filled by a father's love. Like a quilt with one of the squares missing, he would be fine but somehow incomplete.

She shook away the thought, feeling guilty. She would only admit to herself that single parenthood was a lot harder on her than on Brian.

Trolling for a parking space, she pulled into a spot adjacent to the ball fields. The lot was filling up fast with vehicles from all over. Amazing, to think so many people were interested in this strange fund-raiser. She spotted a number of rental cars and vehicles with out-of-state plates. Plenty of these were sleek and expensive late models. The organizers of the auction—ranch owner Lindsay Duncan and director Rex Trowbridge—must be well connected.

Or maybe the brochure didn't exaggerate the success of the various bachelors. But really—an auction?

A couple of news vans had set up, bundled cords snaking along the ground toward the arena where the auction would take place. Some of the bachelors had celebrity status, attracting local and national media. It was the fantasy angle they were after, she supposed. The idea that women were about to compete—publically—for a date with one of these guys.

She shouldn't have been surprised when someone shoved a microphone under her chin and demanded her name as soon as she stepped out of the truck. But she was so taken aback that she blurted, "I'm Twyla McCabe."

"What do you hope to find here today, Miss Mc-Cabe?" the reporter asked, his voice an aggressive, rapid-fire staccato.

"Men," she said ironically. "Lots of men."

"Would that be for a weekend fling, or are you husband-hunting?"

"What?" Lord, did he really think she was serious?

"Think you'll find husband material here?"

She couldn't help herself. She burst out laughing. "Oh, sure. I'm going to snag a millionaire. Or at least a hunky cowboy, one with great pecs and a tight butt."

"Then what words would you use to describe the mood today—*excited, romantic, hopeful?*"

Finding her composure at last, she pushed the microphone away. "You could use them, but you'd be wrong. With a wink, she added, "Try *bold* and *lusty.*"

The busy, sweating reporter gave up and scurried away in search of a more promising scoop.

"Who was that guy, Mom?" Brian asked, getting out of the truck.

"I have no idea, but I'd better wind up on the editing room floor." She opened the tailgate of the old pickup. "Okay, sport, you can help carry." She handed him the raffle box and took the quilt, carefully wrapped in a dry cleaner's bag. It was the best work ever done by the

Converse County Quilt Quorum. Done in a classic log-cabin pattern and made of soft, worn, hand-me-down cottons in a rainbow of colors, it was sure to fetch a handsome number of raffle entries.

She set the quilt on the tailgate and got out the folded card table. Awkwardly, she took the table under one arm and the quilt under the other and started toward the covered pavilion. "Brian, watch where you're going," she called to him as a Ford Explorer with rental plates nosed into the parking lot.

The metal leg of the card table scraped her shin and she set her jaw to keep from cursing. It was hot, she was perspiring, she hadn't made it to the arena, and she was already getting cranky.

"Can I help you carry something?"

She stopped walking and turned to see a tall man getting out of the black sport utility vehicle. For a second, a dazzle of sunlight striking the windshield made her squint painfully. Then he came toward her and her grateful smile froze on her face.

It was him. The guy from the brochure. And not just any guy, but the one in the tux with the long-stemmed rose.

He wasn't wearing a tux and carrying a rose at the moment, though. He managed to look immaculate, casual and foolishly expensive in khaki slacks and a navy golf shirt. A gold watch gleamed on his wrist. He had black hair, white teeth and the sort of unbelievably handsome face you saw on prime-time TV.

"Um, yes, thanks. Maybe you could get this table?"

His cool, dry hand brushed her hot and sweaty one as he took the folded table from her. Brian watched, shading his eyes and staring unabashedly up at the man.

"I'm Brian. Brian McCabe. I have a loose tooth."

"Congratulations," the man said. "Rob Carter. Pleased to meet you, Brian. You too, ma'am."

Twyla knew his name perfectly well. Robert Carter, M.D. He was a Leo whose favorite song was "Misty" and whose ideal woman was Grace Kelly. His idea of a great time was a round of golf at Pebble Beach.

"Twyla McCabe," she said, falling in step with him. "And don't call me ma'am. I'm too young to be a ma'am."

"I'll remember that."

"I call you ma'am when I'm in trouble," Brian pointed out.

"Does that mean I'm not in trouble?" Rob asked.

"Guess not."

"Hot dog."

Brian laughed, clearly intrigued. "Not yet, anyway."

"I'll mind my manners." He was taller than he'd appeared in the brochure, with the long, lanky build of a college basketball player. And Lord, so obscenely good-looking she had to force herself not to stare. The haircut alone would run about a hundred dollars in the city. His cologne was probably something she couldn't pronounce or afford. It was like being in the presence of an alien life-form.

"Twyla," he said, trying out her name. "I've never met anyone called Twyla before."

"My granddad named her," Brian explained helpfully. Though he'd never known his grandfather, Gwen told him family stories each night as she stitched her quilts in her little sitting room. The stories always depicted a dreamer—and they always ended happily. Brian was too young for the truth.

Robert Carter, M.D., had a dazzling smile on his face as he looked down at her. "You don't say."

"I just said so!" Brian objected.

"A figure of speech." Carter's laugh was smooth, gentle, infectious.

Yet Twyla didn't feel like laughing. He made her conscious that her truck's air conditioner hadn't worked in three years, that her cotton sundress was plastered to her back by sweat, and that she hadn't bothered with perfume after her shower today.

Intimidating, that's what he was. And too... everything. Too handsome, too smoothly friendly, too glib, too perfectly put-together, too male.

A pavilion had been set up for the barbecue. The smoky smells of sizzling ribs, chicken and beef filled the air. A PA system blared a sentimental country-and-western song. The young residents of Lost Springs raced around, playing chase with the visiting children.

"Hey, there's Sammy," Brian exclaimed, pointing at a dark-haired kid climbing a tree in the playground. "Can I go, Mom? Can I?"

She nodded. "I'll come find you when it's time for the picnic supper."

"See ya," Carter said as Brian handed him the raffle box and sped away.

"We can set these down here," Twyla said, indicating the spreading shade tree by the rodeo arena. Another volunteer had strung up the hospital guild banner: Converse County Hospital—35 Years Of Sharing And Caring.

"You work at a hospital?" Carter asked her, laying the table down and prying up each metal leg.

"Just as a volunteer once a week." She considered offering him an opening to tell her what a big, important city doctor he was, but decided against it. He was too perfect as it was. He certainly didn't need any prompting from her. "I do hair for a living," she said, almost defiantly.

He set the table on its legs and jimmied it back and forth until it stopped wobbling. Then he looked up at her, hands braced on the table, the nodding boughs of the tree framing his broad shoulders. "Twyla's Tweezers," he said softly. "Now I remember where I've seen that name before."

"It's the Tease 'n' Tweeze," she corrected him.

"Why the Tease 'n' Tweeze?"

"Because that's pretty much what we do."

"And people pay you for this?"

"That's right." A flush stung her cheeks. Just for a moment, she wished she could say, "I sculpt male nudes for a living," or "I'm a district attorney," but the truth was she was a hairdresser and Brian's mom, and she could do a lot worse than that.

He made no comment, but she thought perhaps his smile got a little hard around the edges. Probably so. Men generally didn't find much in common with hairdressers.

"Thanks for your help," she said, unwrapping the quilt.

"No problem." With a casual wave of his hand, Robert Carter, M.D., walked toward the pavilion, putting on a pair of aviator shades.

She taped the raffle ticket sign to the edge of the table. Then she unfolded the quilt and took out some clothespins, stepping back and eyeing one of the tree branches.

She should have asked him to help her hang the quilt. His height would have been a convenience, but now she'd have to reach the branch without him. Standing on tiptoe on the metal raffle box, she pegged a corner of the quilt around the branch.

The second corner was more of a challenge. She reached out, stretching, and too late felt the metal box tip. "Whoa," she said, grabbing the tree limb as the box tumbled away. Dangling absurdly from the branch, she wished she hadn't worn her high-heeled sandals today. Dropping even the short distance to the ground would probably sprain her ankle. Just what she needed—a fat doctor's bill and time away from work.

Grumbling under her breath, she hoped no one could see her predicament. She had her back to the crowd, so she couldn't tell. She was about to let go of the branch, bracing herself in case her ankle snapped like kindling, when a pair of hands grasped her from behind and lifted her down.

"She teases, she tweezes, she swings through trees with the greatest of ease," said Robert Carter, M.D., affecting a newsreader's voice.

"Very funny." Twyla pulled her dress back into place.

"Much as I liked the view," he said, "I wasn't too sure about watching you fall out of a tree."

Twyla leaned her forehead against the rough tree trunk. "This is pretty much the most humiliating thing that's happened to me since Mrs. Spinelli's hair turned out lime green."

"Yeah?" That easy laugh again. He picked up a clothespin and pegged the quilt in place. "I guess that must've been pretty embarrassing."

"You have no idea." She glanced ruefully at the top-pled metal box. "Actually, now you probably do."

He handed her a sweating plastic cup of iced lemon-ade from the table. "I thought you might be thirsty, so I went and got this."

"Bless you." She took a gulp and sent him a grateful smile. "This is awfully good of you."

"You say that with some surprise."

"Do I?"

"Uh-huh. Does it surprise you when a strange man does something nice?"

She laughed. "It surprises me when any man does something nice."

He took off his sunglasses. "I hope you're kidding."

"Beauty parlor humor," she confessed with a wry smile, and finished her lemonade.

Carter studied the quilt for a minute. "So this is what you're selling?"

"Raffle tickets. This is what the winner gets." She fingered the edge of it. "The ladies who make these do wonderful work." She truly loved quilts. Each one was a small, homey miracle in its own unique way. "I think it's amazing how old, tattered pieces of hand-me-down fabric can be stitched together into something so beautiful." She ran her hand over a square. "This could have been some old man's work shirt. This flowered one looks like a grandmother's apron, probably full of holes or burn marks from the oven. Each one on its own was a rag, not worth keeping. But when you take a small piece of this one and a small piece of that one, and stitch them together with care, you get the most magnificent pattern and design, something that will keep you warm for a lifetime."

"Wow," he said, reaching into his back pocket and taking out a slim leather wallet, "that's some sales pitch."

She laughed incredulously as he held out a hundred-dollar bill. "I don't have change for that."

"I don't want change. I want a hundred raffle tickets."

She mouthed "a hundred" even as her stomach lurched with gleeful greed. The hospital guild was usually lucky to pull in seventy-five dollars on a quilt raffle. "Whatever you say," she replied, taking the money. She counted out a hundred tickets from the long, printed roll in the metal box, tearing the strip apart in the middle.

"You hang on to these, and listen for your number when we do the drawing."

He shook his head. "You keep them. I'll check in later. Today might be my lucky day."

"But—"

"I trust you."

"That's what my best customers say."

He put the sunglasses back on. "I'd better go. I think they're getting ready to start."

"Start?" she asked stupidly. This guy was too perfect, and she was pretty certain that all the staring she was doing at him had caused her IQ to drop.

"The auction." He stuck his thumb in his belt, studying her. "Think you'll be bidding on a date, Twyla?"

He sounded like that reporter had earlier. A blush spread over her neck like a rash. "Do I look like the sort who has to buy a date from a stranger?"

"You never know." He indicated the quilt. "Do I look like the sort who has to buy a blanket from a hairdresser?"

"Quilt," she said. "It's a quilt."

CHAPTER FOUR

THE STRANGE ENCOUNTER with Twyla McCabe preoc-
cupied Rob when he should have been trying to have a
good time. It was pretty entertaining, meeting guys he
hadn't seen in years, discovering how they'd turned out,
visiting with teachers he'd had and counselors from the
ranch. He felt a little self-conscious sitting at a long picnic table with a few of the guys, because women kept
walking past, checking them out, whispering and giggling like schoolgirls.

Hanging out with some of the guys made him wonder
about others, the ones he didn't see here today—those
who hadn't made it through to the other end of the tunnel.

A tunnel was the image he thought of when he remembered the past. His early childhood had been a
sunny, idyllic time he recalled only in bright, cartoon-
colored flashes. His mother had been fun. That was what
he remembered about her—laughter, playfulness, tenderness and forgetfulness. She'd let him stay up late and
miss the schoolbus. Her friends and her music were loud,
and meals all came in disposable containers. From the
perspective of adulthood, he realized she had been impossibly young, uneducated, careless—and ultimately ir-
responsible.

Then came the tunnel, the long, dark years he had

spent struggling through a sense that he had been abandoned due to some fault of his own.

Right or wrong, that perception had driven him to excel at everything he attempted. Sports and studies had pulled him closer and closer to the subtle glimmer of light at the end of the tunnel. But the truth was, he hadn't reached the end yet. Emerging as valedictorian from the local high school hadn't caused him to burst into the light. Nor had getting a full scholarship to Notre Dame. Or medical school at Baylor. Or the partnership in his Denver practice.

Maybe the end of the tunnel would be Lauren DeVane and the life they would one day share—as soon as they decided to talk about the future. Lauren, so beautiful she made the rest of the world look profane, inhabited a rarefied world that glowed with the light of its own brilliance. A world where boys weren't abandoned by their underage mothers. Where kids weren't scared of the dark. Where elegance and style softened the sharp edges of life. Being with Lauren made him feel closer to that world—though never actually a part of it.

His plate loaded with barbecue, he took a seat with some of the others, but his gaze strayed to the playground. The equipment had changed. The peeled-log forts and jungle gyms looked a lot safer than the seesaws and nickel pipes they had played on as boys. He recognized Twyla's son Brian on a tire swing. The boy had twisted the chain as far as he could and was now whirling in a full, fast spin, his head thrown back, laughing with wild abandon. Just watching him brought a smile to Rob's lips.

Lauren didn't want kids. They had discussed it at length, and both agreed that they loved travel and spontaneity too much to devote the time and commitment it took to raise a family. It was funny, he mused, watching Brian wind up for another wild ride; they had discussed their feelings about having kids without discussing their feelings about getting married. He had never proposed, nor had she. It was a logical next step in their relationship, yet neither felt pressured or in a hurry to take that step.

Brian stopped spinning and staggered to the edge of the playground. One glimpse of his gray-green face told Rob the inevitable was about to happen.

"Be right back," he said to the others, getting up and walking fast across the playground.

"Gross," a boy said. "Brian hurled chunks." A few of the others, being boys, gathered around, echoing a chorus of "Gross!"

"Hey, Brian," Rob said, taking out a handkerchief. "Got a little motion sickness there?"

Brian stayed bent over, hands on his knees, the back of his neck pale and clammy with sweat. "Uh-huh," he said miserably.

Rob felt awkward as he put his hand on the boy's shoulder and mopped his face with the handkerchief. Briefly, he had considered specializing in pediatrics, but he'd opted for pathology instead. He didn't think he had the patience or the special tenderness it took to deal with little kids. Brian looked completely forlorn, so Rob took him to the men's room and had him rinse his mouth and wash his hands and face.

"Let's go find your mom," he suggested.

On the way to the raffle table, he stopped and got a cup of ice water for the kid. Twyla didn't see them approach. Standing behind her table, she talked to a long-haired guy in blue jeans and a leather vest. She was smiling as she spoke to him.

There were some obvious reasons why Rob had noticed her and why he'd had an intense reaction to her. A great figure and abundant red hair. It was probably out of a bottle, but since she was a hairdresser, she'd know the best way to make it look natural. Or maybe it was natural. Brian's fiery red hair had to have come from somewhere.

She wasn't wearing a wedding ring. He'd noticed that right off.

Yet he felt more than a strong physical attraction to her. He had seen more gorgeous women before, had held them in his arms, taken them to his bed. But there was something about Twyla that went deeper than good looks. She had the most expressive face he had ever seen, eyes that hid nothing. When they spoke, he sensed an easy rhythm between them that worked. In one conversation she struck him as funny, sad, irreverent, practical, unassuming and proud. And self-deprecating.

She laughed at something the ponytail guy said. She hadn't laughed like that for Rob. As soon as the thought formed, he felt like an idiot. What did he care about who made her laugh?

She noticed him coming toward her, and the laughter stopped. Her expression held a peculiar sweetness, and the way she looked down at her son, stroking his hair and brushing her knuckles over his forehead, evoked a strange and haunting reminder in Rob of a distant, dreamlike moment in the past.

He stepped back, frowning. This he didn't need. Trips down memory lane had never held any appeal for him. He had to stay focused on his goals and his future. The sooner he got this auction thing over, the better.

"Hey, sport," Twyla said, all her attention on Brian. "Did something happen?"

"I hurled," Brian said glumly, sipping his water.

She glanced up at Rob. "And the medical term for this would be…?"

He was intrigued that she seemed to know he was a doctor. Apparently she'd looked over his bio. "Acute temporary emesis. Induced by vertigo."

"Otherwise known as…?"

"Spinning on the tire swing until he puked. He'll be fine. Have him sit in the shade for thirty minutes or so."

"Are you going to bill me for this?"

He grinned. "Only if I don't win the blanket."

"Quilt. It's a quilt. The pattern is called Log Cabin."

"We'd better get going, Rob," said the guy with the ponytail.

It took Rob a few seconds to recognize him as another former Lost Springs resident. "Hey, Stan. Good to see you here."

A wail of electronic feedback obscured Stanley Fish's remark. Rob shaded his eyes in the direction of the arena. "They're ready to start."

"I think you're right."

He felt a sudden, idiotic jolt of nerves. How had he let Lauren and her old school pal Lindsay talk him into this? He made himself look nonchalant as he nodded to Twyla. "See you around," he said. "Brian, don't get on any more spinning tire swings, okay?"

As he and Stan walked away from the table under the spreading oak tree, he said, "So you're here for the meat market, too, right?"

"Nope, I came to cover the event."

"Cover—"

"I work for *Clue Magazine*."

"Great. You mean this is going to show up in a national magazine?"

"Hey, why not? It's human interest. People live for stories like this. Mystery dates. Lost boys making good. Women getting into bidding wars over men."

"Then do me a favor. If you quote me, call me an 'unnamed source'."

Stan scribbled something in a pocket notepad. "You wish."

A young woman draped in camera equipment and wearing a vest with rows of pockets joined them. "Hey, guys."

"Rob, this is Betta, my photographer."

Rob greeted her. "So what do you think of a bachelor auction?"

"Sounds like a hell of a good time to me," she said, pulling down the bill of her baseball cap to shield her eyes from the sun. "I always did like shopping."

"Rob, I'm going to put you down as the reluctant bachelor. Hey, that's got a nice ring to it." Stan scratched in his notebook. "So why're you here?"

"Because the place was home to me for eleven years." Rob didn't elaborate. But whatever love and esteem he'd gotten in those years, he'd gotten right here. And as much as that was, it had never been enough. "I came back as a favor to a friend of a…friend." No point in dragging Lauren's name into this. The press knew who she was because of her family.

"So, you looking forward to being sold off as a dream date?"

"Like a root canal, pal. Like a root canal." He went toward the arena where the auction would take place. Rex and Lindsay ran around with clipboards like a couple of soccer coaches. Lindsay's uncle, Sam Duncan, a retired coach and counselor, waved his cowboy hat in an attempt to round up the bachelors. A huge crowd filled the open-air risers—mostly women. Some of the guys were already present, seated in folding chairs around the auctioneer's podium. They laughed and joked and punched one another in the shoulder, remembering old anecdotes from their days here. Rob took a seat by Cody Davis. He looked out at the busy, babbling audience and leaned over to say, "Are you as freaked out by this as I am?"

"Oh, yeah." Cody hooked his cowboy boots around the legs of his chair and balanced it on its hind legs. "Where'd all these females come from, anyway?"

"All over, I'm told." From behind his shades, Rob scanned the rows of bleachers. "Damn, that's a lot of women." They came in all shapes and sizes, all ages and persuasions. There were women in skin-tight western-cut jeans, some of them whistling and hooting good-naturedly as a couple of the guys postured for the audience, flexing their muscles and goofing around. A tall blond woman in jeans and a denim work shirt looked as if she had just stopped in and wasn't certain she wanted to stay. Another sat with two small children, pointing at the risers and appearing to have a serious conference with the kids. A pregnant woman clutching the bachelor auction brochure to her chest sat alone—now there was a scary prospect.

Four women had planted themselves in the center of the front row. The two older ones wore spangled jogging suits and shiny sneakers. Another had golden hair teased high and was smoking a cigarette, and the petite Asian woman next to her looked completely enthralled with the entire situation.

Rob leaned back in his chair and folded his arms. "You know," he observed, "there really is no such thing as an ugly woman."

Davis nodded readily. "That's a fact. That is a fact."

In a trained, booming voice, the auctioneer greeted everyone and laid out the rules of the event. Rob barely listened. There was a sense of absurdity about the whole thing that made it feel not quite real, as if this were a world set apart from everywhere else.

In a way, Lost Springs had always been that. A group of homeless boys whose families had failed them. This was the place where they had come together, where they had fought and cried and raged and laughed and learned. The ranch stood for hope and healing. Letting it close was not an option. That was why he was here. That was why he had agreed to go through with this lunacy. This was a place worth saving, because without it, boys like the boy he had been would have nowhere to go.

Lauren was adamant about doing charitable works. She belonged to a family so wealthy that fifty years ago they'd created a foundation for their charity. The De-Vane Foundation employed a dozen staff members, and Lost Springs had been on their list for years. Rob had met Lauren at another Lost Springs fund-raiser, that one a fairly tame charity ball. The DeVanes were acquainted with the Fremonts of Lightning Creek, and Lauren had gone to boarding school with Kitty Fremont and Lindsay Duncan.

It constantly amazed him that they wound up together, for they couldn't be more different. The heiress and the orphan. Oliver Twist and Princess Grace. Every once in a while, Rob felt an unbidden twinge of discomfort with Lauren. It was hard to define, but the feeling was there, tangible yet hidden, like a pebble in his shoe. She had always been proud of his success and his prospects. But he suspected that deep down she wished he'd been born with real class.

He dismissed the feeling. Sure, they came from different worlds, but they were smart enough to minimize their differences. She was exactly what he had envisioned, when the organizers had made him specify the ideal woman for the auction brochure: an "educated city girl with a high-powered, socially responsible career."

Spying an upswept crown of blond hair in the audience, he felt his heart give a momentary lurch. No, it wasn't Lauren, but a part of him would have been ridiculously pleased to discover she couldn't stand for him to be auctioned off to a stranger and had come rushing up here to buy him for herself.

That would have been pure fantasy and so completely unlike Lauren that it was ludicrous.

"So who do you want to bid on you?" Davis asked. "Got any preferences?"

Before he realized what he was doing, Rob looked directly at the back field, where a tall spreading oak tree nodded in the summer breeze. Twyla McCabe stood by the breeze-stirred raffle quilt, hands on her hips, watching the proceedings with mild bemusement. Then he caught himself and focused on the bleachers. "No preference. Like I said, all women are beautiful. It's for charity, anyway."

"...do this in alphabetical order, I guess," the auctioneer was saying. "So, ladies, put your hands together for our first bachelor, Dr. Robert Carter."

Damn. With jerky, mechanical movements Rob made himself stand. Okay, this was his turn to help out the boys ranch. There was no place for bashfulness or seriousness in this.

From somewhere deep inside, he summoned a wide, welcoming grin and took Lindsay's hand, gallantly bending over it and lifting it to his lips. A chorus of sighs gusted from the audience, and he laughed.

The auctioneer gave a rundown of Rob's bio, making him sound a lot more interesting than he was, eliciting oohs and aahs at his achievements in sports and academics. He'd filled his bachelor questionnaire with facts about his pathology lab, but they hadn't used any of it. Apparently isolating lethal viruses and staving off epidemics wasn't considered "sexy."

"And here's a little something extra, ladies," the auctioneer said. "He's got the soul of a poet."

Rob frowned. Where had that come from?

The auctioneer took out a yellowed piece of wide-ruled writing paper. Rob craned his neck to see. The page was covered in painstakingly neat penciled lettering, and at the top, a gold foil star gleamed. "This was provided by Mrs. Theda Duckworth, former third-grade teacher of Lander Elementary."

Rob's mind careered back through the years. He remembered Mrs. Duckworth as stern, down-to-earth, loving. Big on penmanship. But he couldn't for the life of him recall anything he had written for her.

"It's something Rob wrote when he was just knee-high to a grasshopper, and here's what that boy had to say. 'When I grow up I want to be someone's daddy. I'm told this is not hard to do, but I don't know for sure.'"

A ripple of amusement swept the audience. Rob's grin froze. If this sort of thing was supposed to up the stakes, they were nuts. Who wanted to hear the naive ramblings of a nine-year-old kid?

"'The father in the family fixes things,'" the auctioneer continued. "'Mostly the car, but stuff in the yard and the house, too. Every father is real strong. But it takes a mother and the kids to make him into a father. This is something I better think on a lot more.'"

The women in the bleachers laughed and clapped and "awwwed" at the nauseatingly cute story. Rob tried not to let his chagrin show. He tried to appear relaxed and friendly as the auctioneer opened the bidding.

"Who'll give five hundred dollars for this fine specimen of a man?"

A hand shot up in the bleachers.

"Five hundred dollars, I have five. Who'll bid six?"

Jeez, Rob thought as the auctioneer droned on. Hadn't slave auctions been outlawed by Lincoln?

More hands flashed up so quickly he couldn't tell who was bidding. The bids climbed fast and steep, the women laughing and hollering as they egged one another on.

"Twelve hundred dollars! Do I hear thirteen?"

Rob broke out in a sweat.

His attention darted from one bidder to the next. The denim-shirt girl. The big-hair lady. The mom with two kids. The pregnant woman. A New York–type all in black. The lizard-boots-and-Rolex-watch woman. The silver-haired old lady. Damn, old lady?

Rob wished for a beer. Bad.

The money soared to unreal heights. Nine thousand, ten, twelve. Rex and Lindsay sure knew some free-wheeling folks. Denim Shirt kept outbidding Big Hair. One of the Fremonts made a bid. Then there was a lightning exchange between Lizard Boots and Silver Hair.

Rob wondered if praying would help. He caught himself glancing, somewhat desperately, in Twyla's direction. He found no sympathy there. She rolled her eyes and laughed at the whole idiotic thing. But it calmed him, somehow, catching her eye. She was like a serene center of sanity in the midst of madness. But she kept laughing at him.

"Going once, going twice, going three times...sold," the auctioneer barked, "to Sugar Spinelli, right there in the front row!"

Twyla McCabe, who had been laughing, staggered back against her folding table and clapped her hand over her mouth. Even from a distance, Rob could see her face go pale.

His jaw dropped as the winning bidder gave a shout of victory. Thunderous applause sounded. The bidder and her friend stood up and hugged each other. Spangled jogging suits—one pink, one lavender—flashed in the sunlight.

Rob blinked with disbelief. In his wildest dreams, he hadn't expected this. The highest bidder for his charms...was a gray-haired grandma.

CHAPTER FIVE

ROB FELT COMPETELY buoyant with relief as he left the dais. Behind him, the auctioneer chose a new victim and started describing his charms while the hooting and hollering of the audience started up again. Rob's part was over. But he still wanted that beer.

The jogging-suit ladies went to settle up with the auction officials, so he made his way to the concession stand, savoring a cold beer from a keg. Then he took a cellular phone out of his pocket and dialed Lauren's number.

When she answered, he couldn't contain his laughter. "I think you've lost me forever."

"You mean the auction is over? So soon?"

"My part, anyway."

"So tell me." He could picture her curling up on her black suede sofa and wished like hell he could curl up with her. "I want to hear everything."

He took a sip of his beer. "Okay, they made me go first."

"Because you're worth the most, darling."

"Because it was alphabetical," he said with a wry smile. "Anyway, the bidding went round and round, but you'll never guess who I ended up with."

"I don't want to guess. Just tell me."

"Somebody named Spinelli. Yeah, I think that's her name."

"Sugar Spinelli?"

"You know her?"

"Oil money. Scads of it. Everyone knows her."

"Lauren, your 'everyone' isn't quite the same as my 'everyone.'" He knew she didn't mean to, but when she said "everyone," she gave it a slightly exclusive emphasis. Excluding people like Rob.

"She's ancient, Rob. Why on earth would she bid at a bachelor auction?"

"Beats me. I figure maybe she wants a grandson for a day." The jogging-suit ladies finished with the auction officials and came toward him, chattering away as they neared the pavilion. "I think I'm about to find out," he said to Lauren. "Call you later."

He set down his beer and put on his best smile. "Ladies," he said. "How do you do?"

"We're fine, Robert," said Mrs. Spinelli. "May we call you Robert?"

"Please. It's Rob."

"Used to be Robbie," the other lady, the one in the pink suit, said.

That caught his attention. He studied her hard for a moment. A cloud of bluish-white hair. Square wire-rimmed glasses. A face that held a winning combination of maternal softness, youthful mischief and something else. Steely determination.

"Mrs. Duckworth!"

"Well, thank goodness. I didn't think you'd recognize me."

"It's been a long time." He stood awkwardly for a moment, at a loss. How did you greet your ex-third-grade teacher? Did you call her ma'am? Offer to clean the erasers for her?

She took the decision away from him, opening her arms. "I daresay you've changed more than I."

Rob gave her a brief hug, then stepped back, feeling awkward again. "Thank you," he said to Mrs. Spinelli. "Your generosity was incredible. I know the ranch will put your gift to good use."

"Honey," she said with a wink, "I intend to put you to good use."

His blood ran cold. For a second, he thought she meant…Lord, no way.

Mrs. Duckworth must have recognized the panic in his face. She took him by the arm and led him away from the concession area. "Sugar, we'd better get on with the plan so Robbie can make his arrangements."

"Arrangements?" he asked stupidly.

"For your date."

Oh, man. "And this date would be…?" he asked cautiously.

"Land sakes, not with us." Mrs. Spinelli laughed. "Did you hear that, Theda? Isn't he precious?" She took his other arm. "Dear boy, you're charming, but not our type. This date is with someone else. Someone very special."

His imagination went into overdrive. Maybe she had a psychotic daughter who'd been through a string of husbands. Or a loony niece desperate for a man….

"I'm listening," he said, trying to look calm.

"You're going on a dream date," Mrs. Duckworth said.

"It's all arranged," Mrs. Spinelli added. "Right down to the last detail."

He began to feel a little better, conjuring pictures of an ocean cruise, a night of dinner and theater in the city, a round of golf at a country club—

"To a high school reunion," Mrs. Spinelli added.

The pictures crumbled to dust in his mind. Swaying palm trees gave way to crepe paper garlands draping some smelly gym. "Okay, let me get this straight. I'm taking somebody to her high school reunion."

"Next weekend," said Mrs. Duckworth. "It will be quite marvelous, you see. It's being held at a town near Jackson, so you'll have to fly there, but that won't be a problem. We've already reserved seats on the commuter flight and we've booked the accommodations."

"But you just…bought me," he objected, feeling suspicious.

"Oh, dear, there was never any question that you would be the one. We read all about you in the catalog," said Mrs. Spinelli. "She picked you out right away. I think it was that Armani tux."

"No, the rose," Mrs. Duckworth said. "The single red rose he was holding, Sugar. Don't you think that was what pushed her over the edge?"

Lauren, he thought, hope soaring. Lauren had set this up as some sort of weird practical joke. She had been the one who insisted on the tux and the rose for his catalog picture. She knew Mrs. Spinelli. She was having fun with him, putting these ladies up to this.

"Now, there's something we should clarify right off." Mrs. Spinelli aimed a stern look at him. "This is important. You have to pretend to be engaged."

Rob laughed. It really was Lauren, then. Maybe she wasn't as indifferent about marriage as he thought she was. Maybe she wanted to move their relationship to the next level. "Engaged, huh?"

"Oh, certainly."

Enough of the dancing around. "All right, so Lauren put you up to this."

The ladies exchanged a glance. Mrs. Duckworth scowled. "We don't know anything about anyone called Lauren. We have no idea what you are talking about."

Something told him they weren't pulling his leg. Did they really mean to send him off to some stranger's high school reunion?

He studied their guileless, church-lady faces. Damn straight they did.

"Sorry, ladies. I don't think that's part of the deal. This was supposed to be a date, not a deception."

"Don't be such a spoilsport," Mrs. Duckworth said in a scolding voice. "You never were any fun as a third-grader. I still remember how you used to hide in the cloakroom during make-believe time."

"This date's all arranged," Mrs. Spinelli added, sounding miffed.

"I don't think it would work out, ma'am." He hadn't meant to call her ma'am, just as he hadn't meant to call Twyla ma'am earlier. It simply slipped out. It was odd, but he felt comfortable and at home with these well-meaning but wrongheaded little old ladies. He didn't want to feel at home with them, didn't want to feel the quiet, cozy unity of this small town. The friendly atmosphere of Lightning Creek had nothing to do with the life he had planned out for himself. The sooner he got back to Denver, the better.

"Look," he said, reaching into his back pocket. "I'll write you a check to cover what you spent today, and we'll call things even."

The older ladies sputtered in protest. As he was looking for a pen, he saw Twyla McCabe coming toward him, the folded quilt draped over her arm. "Good news," she said, holding it out.

"Yeah? I could use some."

"We just did the draw, and you won."

So the day wasn't a total loss. At least he had the quilt to show for it. "Thanks, Twyla."

"You know each other already?" Mrs. Spinelli asked, clasping her hands. "Why, that's perfect. Just perfect."

Rob narrowed his eyes. These ladies might look like Betty Crocker, but they sure as hell weren't all sugar and spice. "What's perfect?"

"That you know each other." Mrs. Duckworth spoke slowly and clearly in her teacher voice. "You can get started right away with your plans."

Rob stared at Twyla McCabe. The silky red hair. Big, soft eyes. Light dusting of freckles. A weary, workaday prettiness and a knockout figure to die for. Everything about her screamed small-town girl.

"It's you then," he said in amazement. "It's your reunion."

"Twyla's ten-year reunion," Mrs. Duckworth proclaimed. "You two are going to have such a marvelous weekend."

"That's the other thing I came to talk about," Twyla said, clearly exasperated.

Rob was stunned. Yet at the same time, without quite knowing why, he put his checkbook away.

THE SUN WAS GOING DOWN as Twyla carried the quilt table to her truck, Brian trotting along beside her. An evening chill sharpened the air, bringing with it a low warble of birdsong and the green scent of fresh-cut grass. She had avoided Rob Carter all the rest of the day, watching the festivities with a sense of nervous energy and impending disaster. Each time he seemed inclined to approach her, she busied herself with some chore or other, even volunteering for a stint at the lemonade booth. Finally, when the last bachelor had been auctioned off, it was time to go.

Brian, who had made a full recovery from the motion sickness, had spent the day playing, eating, shouting and throwing things with his friends. He'd ignored the auction itself, showing no interest or understanding of its purpose. He didn't know what Mrs. Duckworth and Mrs. Spinelli had done. That was fine with Twyla, since she wasn't going to make Rob Carter go through with it, anyway.

Near the end of the auction, Brian had caught an inkling of what was going on. Visiting her at the lemonade booth, he'd asked her, "If someone buys one of these guys, does the guy have to do whatever she says?"

Twyla had smiled. "Within reason."

"For how long?"

"I imagine they work that out between them."

"So they should make the guys stay here and be the dads, right?"

A six-year-old's logic was hard to contradict. She shouldn't have asked Brian, but she did. "You think these boys all need a dad?"

"Yeah."

She hadn't dared to ask the next obvious question: What about you, Brian? Do you need a dad?

She wasn't sure she wanted to know the answer to that.

"Sammy Crowe says Mrs. Spinelli bought that guy named Rob, and that he's supposed to do whatever you want."

"Lucky me," Twyla said. "You got any ideas?"

"Are you kidding?" Brian's face had lit up. "I got a million of them."

She'd tried to subdue his enthusiasm, warning him

that there had been a misunderstanding, but the whole weird situation was hard to explain.

"Church tomorrow, sport," she said now, opening the door to the old Apache, buckling him in and covering him with a blanket. He took out his favorite *Dinotopia* book and opened it, yawning hugely. She knew that within minutes, he'd be sound asleep.

As Twyla walked around the front of her pickup truck, she had the unsettling sense that she was being watched. She caught a daunting reflection in the glass of the windshield, glaringly gold from the setting sun. She set down the folded card table and turned. There stood Dr. Robert Carter with his gleaming dark hair and an expectant half smile, watching her in a way no man had watched her in a very long time—with interest and appreciation and maybe just the slightest hint of tenderness. He looked, she had to admit, exactly like the type of man someone would pay twelve thousand dollars for.

"Look," she said, in a rush to get the words out. "I didn't have anything to do with this crazy idea. I had no idea what Sugar and Theda were up to. I want a date with you as much as I want the heartbreak of psoriasis."

Holding the rolled-up quilt under one arm, he studied her for a disconcertingly long time. He was probably a good doctor, she reflected. He wasn't embarrassed to stare at people.

"I've never been compared to a case of psoriasis," he said.

In her nervousness, she laughed. "I don't mean any insult, it's just—" She broke off, nodding with a lame smile as one of the Quilt Quorum ladies crossed the parking area, eyeing them inquisitively.

"Let's step over here." Rob gestured at the end of

the parking area, where a grassy slope angled downward toward the soccer field.

"There's really nothing to discuss," she said. People were heading home now, a number of them pausing to study her and Rob with open curiosity. Word traveled fast in Lightning Creek.

"Then let's discuss nothing in private." He strode away without looking back to see if she followed.

Twyla brushed a stray lock of hair out of her face. They might as well settle this. He probably wanted to get back to Denver as soon as possible. She checked on Brian—absorbed in his dinosaur book—and followed Rob to the goal end of the soccer field. The western side of the grassy area opened to a heart-stirring view of the distant Wind River Range. With the sun settling low on the broken-backed mountains, the light had a deep red-gold, almost dreamlike quality, spreading in soft fronds over the swaying grasses and sage fields beyond the bounds of Lost Springs.

When Rob turned to her, she felt her heart skip a beat, because just for a moment he was limned in pure amber. The fleeting trick of light and shadow made him seem like a creature not of this place, maybe not even this time, trapped in a jewel that held him separate from the world. Then he moved, holding out his hand, and the strange, fanciful moment passed.

Twyla approached him warily and ignored the proffered hand.

"Over here," he said, showing her to a concrete staircase set into the side of the hill leading away from the field. "Have a seat."

"I guess I forgot," she admitted, "you know your way around Lost Springs."

"Yep."

She had an urge to ask him about his boyhood here. Why had he come? How long had he spent here? Did he remember his family? Had he liked living at the ranch? When he was six, did he wish for a dad?

No. She had no business asking him getting-to-know-you questions. Her purpose was to get rid of him. But politely. He hadn't asked for a pair of matchmaking busybodies to draft him into service. Didn't deserve for his philanthropy to be rewarded by being shanghaied to a class reunion.

She took a seat on the top step, and he sat a couple of steps lower. The scent of sweet grass and wild thyme rode the evening breeze. High over the mountains, a single star flickered to life. The skin on her arms prickled with a subtle chill, and she hugged her knees up to her chest, letting the sundress drape down over her legs.

"I want you to know," she began, "that I don't expect you to do—what Mrs. Spinelli and Mrs. Duckworth want you to do. I didn't put them up to it."

"Maybe you ought to give me a little background. What gave them the idea in the first place?"

"I'm assuming you don't have a fundamental understanding of beauty parlor culture," she said, remembering that day in the salon.

"You're right about that."

"Those two ladies were my first customers when I opened the shop. The first dollar bill Sugar Spinelli ever paid me is hanging in a frame on the wall. They've taken me under their wing, and I love them dearly." She couldn't help the fond smile that curved her mouth. "But sometimes they step over the line. They're convinced I need a life. And they think that means finding a man, and they won't rest until they find me one. Even if it costs them several thousand dollars." She laughed, but painfully, because unbelievably they had done just that.

"You could do worse than have friends like Mrs. Spinelli and Mrs. Duckworth."

"I know, and I'm grateful to them. But this time, they've gone a little too far."

"So what do you want to do about it?"

She tilted her head back and let out a weary breath. One by one the stars were coming out, forming a glimmering canopy of purple twilight. "I've been wondering that myself."

"I suppose they'd get their feelings hurt if you didn't go through with their plan."

"Oh, yeah." She shivered, picturing the censorious looks from her two favorite customers. "It's not the money—Mrs. Spinelli loves charitable causes—but in their minds, this is the perfect plan for me. Their way of pushing me out of the nest. They want me to return in triumph to my hometown, with a guy who has magically appeared in my life like a genie from a bottle."

"A fate worse than death."

She chuckled. "I admit, the fantasy does have a certain appeal. Who wouldn't love to show up at a high school reunion looking as if she'd conquered the world—and snagged a big-city doctor to boot. But I sure as heck can't see myself playing out some elaborate masquerade."

He picked a blade of grass and chewed on the end. He probably didn't mean to draw attention to his mouth, but she couldn't help watching him as he nibbled absently on the blade of grass. "Can I ask you something?"

"Sure." She tried not to stare at his mouth.

"What if you showed up just as you are—business owner, Brian's mom?"

"Lord knows, I don't have anything to hide. But—" She broke off as a faraway feeling swept over her. He was too easy to talk to. She ought to shut up.

"But what?"

"I guess I was like most kids in high school. I dreamed big dreams, had a vision of glamour and success and pictured myself a certain way. Then life sort of…happened to me, and I didn't have a chance to see any of my plans through. I suppose, to be perfectly honest, I would love to show up all spit-shined, a dream date opening doors for me."

"So I'd be your dream date?"

She blushed. "Are you kidding? Look at you. A big important doctor with good manners and good taste in clothes? You're a rare sight in Lightning Creek, I promise you that. Rarer still in Hell Creek."

"Hell Creek?"

"My hometown." She still thought of it that way, despite the brutal events that had occurred there, despite the fact that she hadn't been back in seven years. "Anyway, you'd be the talk of the town."

"Don't always believe what you see." He spoke quietly, staring out at the sky, dark purple now and misted by stars.

"What's that supposed to mean?" Dear God, did he have some awful secret?

"Nothing. I'm basically a boring person."

A long silence. She felt the tension of their unfamiliarity. What did you say to a man you didn't know, a man paid to be your companion?

He drummed his fingers on the concrete step. "You know what?"

"What?"

"We don't have a choice. We have to do this."

She felt her mouth moving, but no sound came out. "Do this. You mean go to my reunion."

"Yeah."

"Do you know where Hell Creek, Wyoming, is?"

"I'm told it's not too far from Jackson."

"Trust me, it's not Jackson."

He stuck his hands in his pockets. "Look, Twyla. I agreed to do this fund-raiser. I set aside time to be somebody's bachelor—for fun, and for a good cause. A lot of people have worked hard on the auction. It wouldn't kill us to hold up our end of the deal."

"I never made a deal with anyone," she said.

"Then make one with me. Right here. Right now. Let's do your reunion."

Never, not in her wildest dreams, had she expected this. She was so taken aback that she looked up into his face and said, "I'll think about it. Call me tomorrow and I'll give you my answer."

CHAPTER SIX

IN HIS ROOM at the Starlite Motel at the north end of town, Rob stared at the silent telephone while his gut churned with regrets. Twyla McCabe had tried her best to do the honorable thing, to let him off the hook, and he'd blown his chance to escape. He ought to call her right now and tell her she was right—it would never work out.

But it wasn't tomorrow yet. Hell, it wasn't even ten o'clock yet. He couldn't call her. He should probably phone Lauren and explain the outrageous proposal the old ladies had cooked up.

The blue glow of the neon star on the motel sign flickered sporadically through the slatted blinds. The almost forgotten hum of the wilderness that lay beyond the parking lot crept past the thin walls of the building—the whir of crickets, the chorus of chirrups from frogs, the occasional cry of an owl.

With idle curiosity, he leafed through the papers and brochures Mrs. Duckworth had handed him. They were in a manila folder labeled Twyla's Ten-Year Reunion.

The ladies had left no fantasy unfulfilled. They'd booked seats on a commuter flight from Casper to Jackson and rented a sport utility vehicle for the weekend of the reunion. The accommodations, according to the brochure, were unbelievably deluxe—a handcrafted fishing lodge called the Laughing Water Lodge on the banks of the river, with two bedrooms, a spa and sauna. It was adjacent to a riding stable on the outskirts of Hell Creek and it belonged to a wealthy Jackson developer who used it as a model home to entice world-weary Californians and rich Texans to put down roots in the area. "Your Wild West Wonderland," the ad copy proclaimed, with a photo of a guy in a cowboy hat toting a bucket of feed across a pristine paddock.

Rob tossed the brochure on the table. He didn't mind an occasional ride on horseback, but he'd never found barn chores particularly fulfilling.

When Mrs. Duckworth had handed him the folder, she'd fixed him with the steely stare perfected by all third-grade teachers. "You have to understand, young man—this has to be wonderful for Twyla."

In case he lacked ideas, she and Mrs. Spinelli had included a laundry list of things he was supposed to do to make Twyla McCabe feel special. She needed a gift— a corsage or even an item of jewelry. He was supposed to dance with her. Take her on a picnic, ride horses with her. They suggested a candlelight dinner, a walk in the moonlight, a glass of wine on the hearth rug in front of the fireplace, breakfast in bed.

"We've done our part," Mrs. Spinelli said. "You have to do yours. No man has made her feel special in years. It's up to you."

No pressure there, Rob thought wryly.

He reached out to pull the drape shut against the flickering neon light. Through the slates of the blinds, he saw a pickup truck with running lights and chrome detailing drive by, probably headed for Roadkill Grill down the street. With one last glance at the phone, he grabbed his key and went outside. It was too late to call Lauren, anyway. He might as well join the guys for a beer at the town's only watering hole.

"Hey, Doc." Chance Cartwright waved at him from the thick plank bar when he walked in. Chance poured a beer from a pitcher and handed it to Rob. "Are we having fun yet?"

"You guys tell me."

"Hey," said Rex Trowbridge, grinning crookedly, "we raised a fortune for the ranch today. Now it's time to raise some hell."

Someone punched in a vintage tune on the jukebox. Jerry Jeff Walker's voice filled the barroom, and the guys got busy thumping one another on the back and teasing one another about the auction. Rob hadn't paid much attention to the other deals that had been cut, but it didn't surprise him to learn that not all the bidding was done out of a sense of fun and philanthropy. Russ Hall was stuck being a daddy for a weekend. Cody Davis was being dragged back to his hometown to be the grand master of a parade, and another poor sucker had to serve as some widow woman's ranch hand.

"So how about you?" Stanley Fish, the reporter, pulled up a barstool. "Let's talk about your hot date." Studying Rob's expression, he added, "Off the record, pal. I'm just being nosy."

"What I want to know is why you weren't up there on that stage today."

"Hey, I'm doing my part. This article will be great publicity for the ranch. Donations'll come rolling in when they see all you fine young men doing your civic duty." Stan took a sip of his beer. "So spill."

Rob took a deep breath. "I'm supposed to take some woman to her high school reunion."

Stan rolled his eyes. "You're kidding."

"I wish I was."

"Jeez, why don't you just spend an evening watching paint dry? It'd be more interesting."

"No shit." Rob drank more beer, thinking about a poorly ventilated gymnasium filled with people he didn't know, overdressed and hugging one another, sucking in their guts, squinting at name tags and talking about the past ten years. Trying, in a way that was so achingly human, to make those years seem better, more important than they really had been.

"Do you know why she'd want to drag you along to a reunion?" Stan asked.

"It wasn't her idea," Rob said. He explained about Mrs. Spinelli and Mrs. Duckworth. He thought about the tacky pink-and-white salon next door. It would be so damned easy to help her. Her friends from the salon were making it easy. "They think they're doing her a favor. They want her to waltz back to her hometown with her head held high and her pride intact."

"Sounds like a B movie." Stan eyed Rob critically. "And she needs you in order to do that?"

"Nope. She doesn't need anything. She's fine."

"Then why?"

"The old biddies, I guess. They want everyone to see Twyla as a big success, even in the marriage department."

"Twyla? Her name is Twyla?" Stan swallowed hard, apparently trying not to spew his beer.

"Yeah, Twyla. You got a problem with that?" Rob asked, annoyed by the third degree. "It's a scheme cooked up by these cute little old ladies."

"So blow the whole thing off."

"No. I said I'd do it."

"Damn. This Twyla must be something else."

He shrugged.

"So what's she like?" Stan persisted.

Rob pictured her big misty eyes, and the way her hand stroked her son's head with unconscious affection. He'd be better off not remembering what it had been like to put his hands on her waist and lower her down from that tree, but he couldn't help it. Though brief, the contact had made a vivid impression on him. She'd felt young and firm, pleasantly damp with sweat. And she'd blushed as only a redhead can blush.

"Let's just say she's no mongrel."

Stan signaled for a refill of their beer mugs. "I suppose there's no harm in being some woman's trophy date for a night, if that would fix things for this Twyla. Let's go have a game of darts."

All the rest of the evening, Rob thought about being a trophy date. Stan was still as smart as he'd been during their school days here. Still knew how to get to the heart of the matter. The truth was, Rob did like fixing things. In his practice, he never let go of a case until he figured out the right answer. If it meant pacing the floors all night, reading huge tomes in the medical library or online, he doggedly looked for answers.

Lauren liked to boast about his deep commitment to his profession, but that always made Rob feel like a fraud. Because deep down, he knew what motivated him, and it didn't have anything to do with high principles and a commitment to the greater good of mankind.

It was as simple as a boyhood memory and a vow to put security first. As simple as his last glimpse of his mother, a pale, pretty woman with tears in her eyes and a bruised jaw. With eerie clarity, he recalled standing in the ranch director's office, intimidated by the big overstuffed leather chairs and the Bierstadt and Remington prints on the walls.

With a schoolgirl scrawl, his mother signed her name to a long document. "You'll be better off this way," she'd said, and three decades later Rob could still feel the dry, warm touch of her hand on his cheek. "I can't give you no kind of life, not now. Maybe later…"

"Maybe later" had haunted him for years afterward. Sundays at the ranch were family day, and Rob used to show up at twelve o'clock on the dot, hair combed and shoes shined, wearing his best jeans. "In case she comes today," he used to tell Mr. Duncan. But she never did.

Even after Mr. Duncan gently suggested that Rob find some other Sunday activity, he kept showing up, kept hoping. He'd sit unobtrusively in the Spruce Room of the main lodge, watching as boys got hugs from families that couldn't keep them yet still cared enough to show up every now and then with a box of chocolates and some comic books.

Rob knew the Duncans kept trying to locate his mother. At the very least, they wanted her to relinquish her guardianship of him so a family could adopt him. But they never found her, and Rob won awards for being at Lost Springs the longest.

As he got older, he tried to reconstruct what Peggy Jean Carter's life had been like. A runaway, she'd had no family to speak of, no education. Jerked around by an abusive man, mishandled by social service agencies. Finally, desperate and broke, she had handed her son over to strangers and walked out of his life.

Maybe if someone had done one kind thing for his mother, she wouldn't have left him all those years ago. She might have found the pride and self-respect to pull herself together and meet life head-on rather than running scared all the time.

Kindness made a difference in the world—that was the enduring lesson of Lost Springs. Maybe that was why he was going to talk Twyla into going to her reunion with him.

ROB AWAKENED to a medley of church bells. He stepped outside his motel room, taking a deep breath. The sky was a brilliant blue, with a brittle intensity that was rare outside this area of Wyoming. It was like being on top of the world or on another planet. The air was so clear, the light so strong.

Going back inside, he showered and shaved and got dressed in jeans and a golf shirt, then stuck his shades in his pocket. Twyla had said to phone her, but that didn't seem right. He needed to see her in person.

After breakfast at the Grill, he started off for the old McCabe place. That was how Reilly, at the feed store, referred to it. "The old McCabe place" sounded quaint, Rob thought, picturing a graceful Victorian house and a manicured lawn.

As he drove up the pitted gravel drive, he shouldn't have been surprised to discover that he was wrong. The mere sight of the property gave him an ominous feeling.

The 1920s wood-frame house was falling apart. Set on the brow of a hill, the place looked worn, the rickety porch rail giving it the aspect of a face in need of dental work. Weathered wood, peeling paint, shutters hanging awry. The only color came from hedges and flower boxes filled with geraniums.

As Rob got out of his car, a small boy and a large dog came racing down the hill at a rough-and-tumble run. The dog gave a sharp, protective bark, but Brian hushed him. "It's okay, Shep. Hiya, Rob."

"Hey, Brian. I came to see your mother. Is she busy?"

"Nope. Me and Mom just got back from church. C'mon in." Brian stomped up the dusty walk.

The porch steps creaked ominously beneath Rob's tread.

"Hey, Mo-om!" Brian called. "Rob's here—that guy Mrs. Spinelli bought for you yesterday." Whistling for his dog, the kid went back outside, the screen door slamming in its frame and creating a shudder that reverberated through the house.

Rob found himself standing in the middle of an old-fashioned vestibule. The place smelled of lemon oil polish and cinnamon and coffee—some would call it the smells of home, but of someone else's home, never his.

He rested his hand on the newel post, dark with age, and the wooden ornament came off in his hand. He swore softly under his breath and was trying to replace it as Twyla came from the back of the house.

"Hi," she said, her expression slightly quizzical. "I wasn't expecting—" She spotted the newel post in his hand.

"Sorry," he said.

"Happens all the time." She fit the peg in place and smiled up at him. "I keep meaning to fix it, but I've never been much good at that sort of thing. Give me a head of hair any day, but home improvement is a complete mystery."

A long, awkward pause stretched out between them. Rob noticed that she was wearing a nice yellow dress—for church, he guessed. He wondered if guys in church stared at her because, damn, she was a knockout with all that red hair and those legs. He tried to think of something else. Like what the hell he was doing here. She had all but let him off the hook yesterday, yet something had driven him to find her, to convince her that they ought to give it a shot. Now that he was here, standing like an intruder in her house, he had no idea what that something was.

A small, white-haired woman came in. She wore a flowered apron over her dress, an unorthodox-looking pair of red tennis shoes and a pleasant smile.

"Mom, this is Rob Carter. Rob, my mother, Gwen."

He shook hands. "Pleased to meet you. I don't mean to intrude on your Sunday—"

"Oh, heavens, Sundays were made for company, weren't they, Twyla dear? We absolutely love having people over. Can I get you some coffee? I've got some cinnamon rolls just out of the oven."

"I'd be a fool to turn down that offer," he said. "Smells delicious."

"I'll give you a hand, Mom."

"Don't you dare. I'll just be a minute."

The two women shared a smile. Sometimes when he saw a parent and child, he felt a raw burning inside him that had no antidote. Long ago he had made a mental list of the things he could never have, like a mother and a father. He had dedicated his life to acquiring the things he *could* have—a good education, a meaningful career, friends he enjoyed. Since meeting Lauren DeVane, he had begun to think a wife was even a possibility.

"Your mom's nice."

"The best." A shadow darkened her face and her smile dissolved, then reappeared quickly. "She lives with us—there's a mother-in-law apartment in the back—and watches Brian when I'm at the salon. She did a lot of the work on that quilt you won.''

Twyla led the way into an old-fashioned parlor. The room had a high ceiling outlined by fancy molding and tall windows hung with lace curtains. The furniture wasn't grand, certainly not priceless antiques, but it seemed to fit. Between the two windows was a small upright piano, polished to a high sheen. Built-in bookshelves were crammed with an eclectic mix of titles. Scanning them, Rob noted a heavy concentration of psychology texts and self-help books on everything from panic attacks to holistic grief recovery. Not what one would expect of a hairdresser. Maybe her mother was the reader.

Deciding it was impolite to speculate on people's reading choices, he turned his attention to the collection of family pictures. Framed photos hung everywhere or stood propped on every available surface. Seizing on a way to fill the silence, Rob said, "So give me the grand tour. These photos don't have captions.''

"It's just family stuff. Boring, really,'' she said.

He picked one up. The photo featured Twyla as a girl, playing outside a double-wide mobile home. "I'll be the judge of that. Humor me.''

"Lord, I was a skinny thing, wasn't I?'' she said. "That's the Lazy Acres Mobile Home Court, where I spent most of my childhood. Classy place.'' With a wry smile, she gave a shake of her head. "Here I am with my father on the miniature golf course he built. He spent all his savings on it.''

"Quite the place.''

She set down the framed photo. "I'm sorry to say it failed despite the marvelous innovation of sound effects. Bells and whistles when the ball went in the hole.''

"He must've been way ahead of his time."

"He was a dreamer," Gwen said, not unkindly. She had entered the room with a tray of coffee and rolls. "And a bit of a dabbler, never settling on one project." She stared fondly at the golf course photo, then wiped her hands on her apron. "I'll leave you two, then."

"No, please, join us—"

She held up a hand. "I promised Brian I'd sugar down those blackberries he picked. We'll have a cobbler tonight."

Rob grinned, watching her go. "Don't tell me. She's in on the matchmaking along with the other two."

Twyla nodded. "I swear, I get tired of it sometimes. They're so convinced I need someone. They've tried to set me up with a tractor mechanic, a cow buyer, a roughstock rider, the sheriff's deputy…and a bunch of others." She smiled a little shyly. "This is the first time they've actually paid for a man to match me up with."

"The pressure's killing me." Rob poured coffee and helped himself to a roll, savoring the fresh-baked taste of it. "So keep going. I want the rest of the tour."

The photos of Twyla chronicled a life that probably should have added up to something different than it had. At the age of thirteen, she stood proudly beside an adjudicator, having won her first local piano competition. She was the cutest cheerleader he'd ever seen, and valedictorian of her high school class. The prom picture was a classic—the oversize corsage, the nervous smiles, the stiff poses. She had learned to speak French by correspondence course and was accepted at no less than four private colleges.

"So did you go?" he asked.

A faraway look softened her face. "I sure wanted to, but things didn't work out."

"Would it be getting too personal to ask what those 'things' were?"

She flinched, pain darkening her eyes. "I got married right out of school to a guy who was a junior in college. We were too young, of course. Every couple that's too young believes they'll be the exception to the statistics—ever notice that?"

"Never really thought about it."

"Have you ever been married, Rob?"

"No." He didn't bring up Lauren. They weren't married or even engaged. They just…were. He finished his coffee, gulping it too fast. "Why do you ask?"

"No reason." She bit her lip, and a troubling emotion glittered in her eyes.

"Hey, you don't have to explain," Rob said quickly. This was exactly why he practiced medicine in a laboratory. He didn't have the patience and compassion to deal with people getting emotional, baring their souls.

"No, I don't mind talking about the past, really."

Great. Rob reminded himself that she had offered him a chance to back out. Instead, like an idiot, he'd shown up at her house. Her poor, decrepit house that smelled of baking bread and furniture polish and rang with the laughter of a little boy.

Her eyes, hazy with remembrance, looked unseeing out the window. "Sorry. I don't mean to be melodramatic. But what happened was big stuff for a small town like Hell Creek."

She took a sip of her coffee and visibly tried to compose herself. She had a great face, Rob thought, watching her. She had the subtle freckles and fair coloring of a natural redhead, eyes that said too much, a mouth that smiled too easily.

Agitated, she stood up, rubbing her hands up and

down her arms as if she felt a sudden chill. "To make a long story short, my father died suddenly and my mother—" she glanced at the doorway and dropped her voice "—was left pretty devastated, emotionally and financially."

Rob suddenly wished he was far away. Very far. "Twyla, are you sure you want to talk about this?"

She stopped rubbing her arms. "Does all this emotional baggage bother you?"

"No," he lied.

"Let me know if it does, and I'll stop."

"You mean there's more?"

She took a sip of coffee. "Stay tuned. Where were we? Oh, yeah. It didn't help that my husband was dumping me right about the time of my father's death. So much for my own plans. I couldn't go away and leave my mother twisting in the wind. Since I already knew how to do hair, I looked for a salon to buy so we could stay together as a family. Practically overnight, I had my own business."

"Twyla's Tease 'n' Tweeze."

A smile curved her mouth as she took a seat. "Call it a moment of mad whimsy. Mom and I were hitting the zinfandel that night."

Family, Rob realized, was a tender trap. When he had graduated from high school, there was no one to stand in the way of his plans. No parent in need or sibling in trouble or lover making demands. He had to wonder if he would have given up his future for the sake of a family member who needed him.

Rob glanced down. In her lap, Twyla had torn a napkin to shreds. "Hey," he said, "I didn't mean to upset you."

She noticed the napkin and shook her head. "Don't

worry. In a town like Lightning Creek, no one has any secrets. I expect the entire membership of the Quilt Quorum knows you're here right now.''

"And is that a problem?''

"No, not at all. But I absolve you of your obligation to go through with this reunion thing.''

"That's what I came to talk about.''

"Good. I'm glad you agree—''

"We're going.''

She laughed, an easy laugh that was indulgent and the slightest bit condescending. He imagined her laughing that way in her salon as her customers enumerated their husbands' quirks.

"Rob, really. That's a nice gesture. But I know how boring it would be for you.''

"I mean it. We're going to your reunion.''

"Why?'' She seemed astonished, vaguely suspicious. "Why are you being such a good guy about this?''

"You have something against good guys?''

"No, I'm just amazed that you're one of them. Most rich doctors wouldn't bother.''

"Thanks for reducing me to a stereotype,'' Rob said. "Look, your little old ladies planned this thing down to the last detail. If we go through with it, maybe the town matchmakers will back off for a while.''

She sat in pensive silence. Rob wondered what it would be like to know her, to be privy to the thoughts behind her light, expressive eyes.

No, he didn't want to know. They'd best remain polite strangers. He wouldn't see her again after the reunion, so there was no need to mess things up with rambling heart-to-heart talks. No need to wonder what might happen if—

He reeled with the thought. People complicated each

other's lives. Twyla McCabe was living proof of that. He didn't need any part of it.

"Would you like to take a walk?" she asked suddenly.

Caught off guard, he said, "Sure."

They walked outside and up the sun-warmed slope at the back of the house. Bees grumbled indolently through the daisies and blue lupine and Indian paintbrush that covered the hill, but Rob found his gaze straying to Twyla.

He kept telling himself to keep his distance, but it wasn't working. He noticed everything about her—the way the breeze lifted her hair, the fact that she wasn't wearing any panty hose, the way her face softened when she looked down the hill and spied Brian and her mother, sorting berries on the railed back porch. There was a certain way a woman had of looking at those she loved. Rob had noticed this during his pediatric rotation. It was the most subtle, soft and tender look he could imagine. Twyla did it so naturally.

She showed him around with the mock formality of a tour guide, and he discovered a shed filled with a treasure trove of tools, a handyman's dream. "The former owner had a woodworking shop," she explained. "Have you ever done any woodworking?"

"Carpentry was part of the program at Lost Springs. I liked it." Rob surprised himself with the comment. He had liked the work, but he hadn't worked with his hands in years.

"I think the owner before him was even more interesting," Twyla said, pointing out an abandoned chicken coop that had concealed a whiskey still in the twenties. She went on to show him a stream trickling from a crack in the rocks on the hillside and a half-buried thresher so rusted and ancient that she had planted it with morning glories and called it a yard ornament.

As he checked out the place with her, he told himself he was looking forward to getting this over with.

But as the moments wore on, soft and drowsy with the flavor of a summer afternoon, Rob felt something happening to him. Against all good sense, against the central tenet of his life's plan, he felt drawn to her.

Drawn to this girl who grew up in a trailer park, nurtured on grand dreams that had no chance of ever coming true. This girl who dyed hair for a living.

As they walked along a beaten earth path that bordered her property, he kept trying to focus on Denver, his plans, his ambitions...Lauren. But his attention kept getting tugged in a different direction altogether. It was nuts. A basic animal attraction. Twyla had the most amazing looks. No guy with eyes in his head could help himself.

And Brian was simply an added distraction. He reminded Rob painfully of himself at six—abandoned at Lost Springs, hungry for a connection, showing up in the Spruce Room every Sunday during family hour, "just in case."

He eyed the weary-looking, paint-thirsty house. There was something sorry and neglected about the property, an air of thwarted plans, aborted possibilities.

This was bad, he told himself. He barely knew this woman yet he wanted to know everything.

He had spent his whole life trying to forget and escape small towns, small farms, small people and their small dreams. So what was he doing back here, finding himself more concerned about Twyla's broken porch rail than anything else in the world?

"We need a game plan," he said, walking to his car.

"What do you mean?"

"For your reunion."

"But I never said I'd—"

"I never asked. I'm telling you."

"Just like a doctor," she said. "Arrogant."

"Now, look. People are going to ask how we met, all that stuff. It would probably be a good idea to coordinate our stories."

She burst out laughing. "Oh, this is so insane, and it's going to be so much fun!"

He looked down into her laughing face, her merry eyes. "You need more fun in your life."

"You're beginning to sound like one of my customers."

"Just stay away from me with your scissors." He grinned. "I'll be up sometime Friday on a flight to Casper. I'll call you during the week. Mrs. Spinelli's travel agent took care of all the bookings to Jackson."

"Oh, God. We're really going to do this, aren't we?"

"Are we ever." He hesitated. Instinct made him want to say goodbye with a kiss. Instead, he handed her a business card. "All my numbers are there."

"Thanks. See you on Friday, then."

As he drove away from the farm, a plume of dust obscuring the view, Rob had a feeling that he had just done something he shouldn't have.

CHAPTER SEVEN

"SOMETHING'S WRONG," Twyla said, scowling at Sadie Kittredge's reflection in the circular rose-tinted mirror.

"It's my usual set." Sadie craned her neck, turning her head this way and that.

"I don't mean your hair," Twyla said. "I mean with this whole thing. This whole reunion thing."

She took a rake and added some loft to Sadie's bright, glossy curls. All week long she had been thinking about going back to Hell Creek, returning like a conquering hero with a trophy doctor at her side. The problem was, she wasn't the conquering-hero type. Or conquering heroine, for that matter.

But a long time ago, she had been. Her father had taught her to dream, and she knew there was magic in dreams. Meeting Rob, facing the challenge of going back home made her want the magic back. It made her want the fire—even at the risk of getting burned.

"Okay, so tell me what you're thinking," Sadie said, "and I'll tell you why you're wrong."

"That's why I love you so much," Twyla said. "What I'm thinking is that I'm such a different person from the one who left Hell Creek seven years ago. I'm too old to play games like this. I shouldn't care what they think of me."

"You're never too old to find validation." Sadie

worked for the county schools as a family therapist, and she was annoyingly good at what she did.

"So what do I need to validate, Herr Doktor?" Twyla asked.

Sadie swiveled herself around in the chair to face her. "The choices you've made."

"Honey, I don't have time to stop for lunch, much less validate my life choices."

"Going back is necessary closure. You've told me enough about the circumstances of your leaving that I understand you left a few loose ends untied."

"That's a diplomatic way of putting it." The truth was, she had fled a town that had humiliated her father, left a husband who had hung her out to dry, and found herself alone with a mother so devastated by events that she couldn't bring herself to leave the house. After a couple of glasses of wine one time, Twyla had confessed this to Sadie, whose eyes had filled with angry tears for the broken young girl Twyla had been and for the panic-stricken Gwen, who had yet to step off the porch of the old McCabe place.

"It's not too late to cancel," Twyla said. "I really should stay. I know Diep can do hair as well as nails, but Saturday's always a big day at the shop, and I've never spent a night away from Brian—"

"You worry too much," Diep Tran scolded, bustling past with a tray of clanking nail supplies. "I keep the salon open, your mother keep Brian, you go to Jackson with Dr. Hunk. No worries, none at all."

"Ha. Easy for you to say." She pumped down the swivel chair and untied Sadie's smock, shaking it out and tossing it into a stainless steel pail. "If I really wanted validation, I'd go alone instead of leaning on Dr. Hunk."

"Why would you want to when you have a willing hunk to lean on?" Sadie asked.

"That's what I mean about something being wrong. He's too willing. There's got to be something the matter with this picture."

"Good God, did you leave your self-esteem hanging on the back of the bathroom door this morning?" Sadie demanded. "Why can't you simply allow the idea that a gorgeous, successful man wants to take you away for a weekend?"

Twyla would never admit it, but just hearing the words made her stomach jump with a forbidden thrill. Maybe he did find her attractive and interesting, though they had so little in common. On the other hand, maybe he was simply a responsible guy who wanted to fulfill his end of the bargain. Every time she was tempted to believe in him, she reminded herself that logic could explain his actions. Best to be practical, she told herself briskly. Hopeless romantics were just that: hopeless.

Diep checked the clock. "No appointments for half an hour. You sit, Twyla. Time to do your nails."

"I never get my nails done," she protested. "It interferes with my work."

"No more working today. You take tomorrow off. Get ready for Dr. Hunk."

"Oh, God—"

"Quit being such a baby." Sadie pressed the small of her back, propelling her to Diep's station. "Do as Diep says and call me tonight. I have to run."

After Sadie left, Twyla sat down and laid her hands on the table. "Okay. I'm all yours."

"Feet first," Diep said sternly. "Shoes off."

Twyla knew she would get no peace unless she complied, so she took off her shoes. The pedicure, she had to admit, was pure heaven. Silky, heated lotion in the foot tub. A massage that made her shut her eyes and groan. Delicate strokes of the brush, applying a perfect seashell pink.

"Too bad it's not a real date," Twyla said. "I wouldn't mind showing off my feet."

"It is a real date. And you better show off your feet," Diep said sternly.

"Maybe I'll wear sandals on the flight to Jackson," Twyla conceded.

"Maybe you go barefoot."

Twyla bit her lip sternly, trying not to picture herself naked…with Rob Carter.

Diep finished, then plucked Twyla's hands out of the heated gloves. "Okay, now the hands."

There were women who drove as far as seventy miles to get their nails done by Diep Tran. When it came to nails, she had no peer. She bent industriously over Twyla's hands, transforming the blunt, workmanlike nails into the elegant, sculptured ovals of a lady. They looked as if they belonged to someone else. To someone who traveled the world, played piano in concert, spoke French to foreign diplomats. To the woman Twyla had once had every intention of becoming.

"What you thinking, eh?" Diep asked, studying her face. "You got a sad look, Twyla."

"I'm not sad. Just remembering the past."

"Past is always little bit sad, for everybody." At the age of three, Diep had made the perilous voyage in a leaky boat from Saigon to international waters, where the fleeing refugees were picked up by a Japanese freighter and left on an oil-drilling platform, then transported to a refugee camp in Indonesia. She never said much about it, but she had lost most of her family members during the migration. "You think about tomorrow, Miss Scarlett."

Diep reached for a bottle of red glitter.

Twyla snatched her hand away. "Oh, no, you don't. No fancy stuff."

"Tasteful fancy stuff. Your dress is red, yes?"

"Yes, but—"

"Shoes are red?"

"Yes—"

"Then hold still and let me work."

Twyla forced herself to relax. She had already resigned herself to taking the plunge. If she was going to become a woman of mystery this weekend, she might as well go all the way. Vanity was permissible in a woman—she had built her business on that premise. But she had always had a personal problem with it. There was probably some deep psychological reason that she enjoyed making other women beautiful but was so ambivalent about herself. Pondering that, she caught herself truly reveling in Diep's attention.

Her reunion dress hung in the clear plastic zipper bag on the back of the office door. Mrs. Spinelli had had it shipped overnight along with shoes and a bag, from Nieman Marcus, and Diep's mother had done the alterations. Twyla knew in her heart the dress was too much, too red, too expensive, but the moment she had put it on, she had known it was the one.

Diep concentrated deeply, using tiny brushes and even a surgeon's blade for the details. When she was finished, Twyla regarded her nails with amazement. Each ring finger was tipped with a tiny, perfect depiction of the ruby slippers.

"It's beautiful, Diep. You're a genius."

"You always say there is magic in the ruby slippers. Now there is magic in your hands."

HEY, STRANGER." Lauren DeVane opened the door of her town house. "Long time no see. I missed you." She lifted up on tiptoe and kissed Rob's cheek.

"Missed you, too," he said automatically, loosening his tie, grateful for the end of a busy day at the lab.

She had been to something called a "trunk show" in San Francisco. He was a little afraid to ask what a trunk show was, imagining a gross anatomy class from his med school days.

"How was your flight?" he asked.

"Fine. What's that, darling?"

He handed her the wrinkled plastic bag. "Something from Lost Springs. The auction wasn't a total loss."

She took out the quilt he had won in the raffle. Just the sight of it, the worn and faded pieces forming new patterns, the hand stitching picking out swirling shapes, reminded him uncomfortably of his first meeting with Twyla McCabe. He'd had a powerful reaction to her, and that wasn't like him.

Lauren tilted her head to one side, silky yellow hair spilling over her shoulder. "A blanket?"

"It's a quilt. I won it in a draw at the bachelor auction."

She unfolded it halfway and eyed the soft blues and pearly pastel colors against her black ultrasuede sofa. "Quilts are so weird. Made out of people's hand-me-down rags."

Rob went over to the wet bar, making himself a whiskey and soda and a vodka martini for Lauren. They touched their glasses, and she said, "Finally we get an evening together. I can't believe you're leaving again tomorrow.''

Friday, he thought with a heavy feeling in his gut. He summoned a smile for Lauren. How tall and elegant she looked, like a Charles Aubrey painting. All she lacked was a cigarette in a twelve-inch holder. "Hey, DeVane, you're the one who put me up to this auction thing. Having second thoughts?''

She laughed and nibbled at the olive in her martini. ''About some girl's ten-year reunion?''

The story of the local oil heiress buying him to take a woman named Twyla to her high school reunion intrigued and amused Lauren. With long, elegant fingers she twirled her martini olive on the end of a toothpick and regarded him with an enigmatic smile. "Your weekend could be very interesting."

He laughed briefly. "Right. I can hardly wait."

"Think about it. This woman was driven from her hometown in disgrace—"

"Why do you think she was disgraced?"

"It makes sense. She left abruptly, abandoned her plans for college, and it takes a bachelor auction to get her to go back. Clearly she's hiding something. I'll bet there's some great dirt she's not telling you."

"Don't count on me to dig it up," he said.

"You're no fun. I wish I could be a fly on the wall."

"Better yet, you go to the reunion and I'll stay here."

"Don't be a baby. Sugar Spinelli never does anything halfway. You'll have a fabulous time, show this poor girl a little glimpse of the high life, and you'll have done your good deed for the day."

Rob took a swallow of his drink. "You make it sound so simple."

She lifted one eyebrow in that funny, cynical way of hers. "Isn't it?"

No.

"I suppose," he said.

"What does she look like?"

Rob smelled a trap. "I don't know. A hairdresser, I guess."

Lauren laughed. "Does a hairdresser look a certain way? Mine has a five-o'clock shadow and a cowboy hat, and his name is Siegfried."

"She doesn't have a five-o'clock shadow."

"You're being evasive." Lauren eyed him sharply. "So what does she have?"

"Red hair. And I know she's about twenty-eight because it's her ten-year reunion."

Lauren lifted one thin eyebrow. "Is she tall or short?"

"Average, I guess. Shorter than you."

"Good figure?"

"Yeah, I guess." Glancing at Lauren, he realized it was the wrong answer. "I didn't pay much attention. She's not huge, she's not skinny. So quit with the third degree."

She finished her drink with a satisfied smile and tucked her stocking feet up under her on the sofa. "You know, darling, the Fremonts have a summer cabin up in Chugwater. That's just a short drive from Lightning Creek. Maybe we could have a rendezvous there after your weekend."

"Sure," he said. Last time they had spent a weekend at a cabin, she'd spent most of her time on the phone. Maybe the Fremonts' place didn't have a phone. "I guess. I—" His beeper went off, and he checked it, muttering a soft curse when he saw the code in the LED screen.

Lauren handed him the cordless phone. "Problem?"

"This referral is driving me crazy. I swear, the patient wants every test done three times."

"I thought I was being smart choosing a pathologist," she said with a pretty pout. "You're not supposed to have crazy hours."

"I usually don't." He dialed his service and listened carefully to the message. Mrs. Lloyd-Morgan, whose tests had all come back negative, was supposed to be a happy camper by now. Instead, she was demanding to speak to him in person.

He had met her once—she was an acquaintance of Lauren's parents. Her face, surgically enhanced by one of Rob's associates over at Cedarview, had been drawn into wan lines as she enumerated her ailments. She was a perfect example of why he avoided patients. Tonight, however, she wanted attention, and she wanted it now. According to the answering service, Mrs. Lloyd-Morgan was demanding a "doctor who wouldn't overlook her suffering."

"I'll have to go into the office for this one," he said, handing Lauren the phone.

"We were supposed to have dinner with the Steins. He's on the board at Cedarview, you know." Lauren knew everybody, and she was determined that Rob should meet them all.

"Sorry. Can you give them my regrets?"

She smiled with a tolerance he appreciated. Damn, he was lucky to have her. "Don't worry about me. I'll make an early evening of it myself. I'm tired after the San Francisco trip." A diamond-encrusted tennis bracelet flashed as she cupped the back of his neck and kissed him. "Call me when you're done."

He went to the door, and she said, "Rob?"

He turned to see her holding out the quilt. "Yeah?"

"Don't forget your blanket."

"It's a gift," he said.

She stuffed it into the plastic bag. "I appreciate the sentiment, darling, but it doesn't go."

MERCIFULLY, Mrs. Lloyd-Morgan's fury was brief and easily assuaged by an assurance that he would perform a battery of expensive, high-level tests in consultation with her internist next week. By the time he finished, it was seven o'clock, still early enough to return to Lauren's. But when he phoned her, the line was busy, so he decided to head home, maybe lose some of his tension on the long walk to his condo. The last sun of the day lay across the landscaped hills of the medical center. The coffee carts and hot dog stands were folding up for the day, and cars crammed the outbound lanes of the avenue.

Without breaking stride, Rob loosened his tie and opened the top of his shirt. What was it with him lately? He seemed to be a magnet for rich hypochondriacs.

Manna from heaven, his partners in the practice would declare. They loved patients like Mrs. Lloyd-Morgan. Diagnose an important-sounding illness, prescribe a nice mild laxative and she declares you Albert Schweitzer.

The trouble was, Rob was beginning to resent the time he spent on patients who had no complaint more serious than boredom or neglect from a busy husband. He had chosen to practice medicine for more than just the money and prestige, though some days he forgot the real reason. It was his dream. He liked getting to the root of a problem, liked the precision and accuracy of lab work. He liked doing something that mattered.

But lately, he felt like an overpaid lab technician. At first, a pathologist's practice had seemed the ideal setup for him. Figure out the problem, pass the course of treatment on to someone who would administer it. But for the past year or so, he had been wondering what it would be like to go into practice as a GP. He'd tried to explain to Lauren that he might want patients who were his to worry about, his to heal. Lauren hadn't understood at all. She loved his flexible schedule—he was free to travel, he didn't have to be on call. It suited their lifestyle perfectly.

Then why didn't it feel right anymore?

His strides lengthened in agitation. It had been a lousy week, that was all—following the strangest weekend of his life. The bachelor auction had left him distracted and out of sorts. He'd get over it. The sooner he got this reunion thing behind him, the better.

He passed through the bustling commercial area of Lower Downtown Denver. Rescued from urban blight, former railroad warehouses had been transformed into a mecca for shoppers, tourists and brew-pub fans. He was tempted to stop in at Champion's for a growler of lager, but passed it by.

A few blocks from his vintage condo on the corner of Drake and Albert, Rob found himself in front of the plate-glass window of Breaknell Designs, staring at a necklace displayed on a field of black velvet. He had passed the jeweler's shop hundreds of times, but he'd never been tempted to look. Today, the window display had caught his eye. Behind him, the smog and bustle of Denver's LoDo district steamed and swelled, but he ignored the familiar rhythm of the city. He just kept staring at the necklace.

Each link in the chain was an oval-shaped setting for a ruby, tapering gradually to a slender thread at the fastening. In the center, the jewel was large and set between a pair of unusual triangular-cut diamonds.

The sound of traffic on hot pavement faded to nothing, because all Rob could hear was the echo of his last phone conversation with Twyla.

What color is your dress?

Red. Ruby red. Mrs. Spinelli wouldn't take no for an answer. I've never owned anything this red in my life.

It was Lauren who had taught him the importance of knowing the color of a woman's dress on a date. In fact, it had been Lauren who had insisted that he ask Twyla about her dress. Lauren even went so far as to suggest a cummerbund color for Rob that would complement the red dress. At first he'd thought she was kidding, but it turned out that this sort of thing actually mattered to most women.

He thought he should probably get Twyla a corsage or something. But when he saw the ruby necklace, he forgot all about a corsage.

With a doomed sense of inevitability, he went into the jeweler's and asked to see the necklace. The price staggered him, though he could easily afford it. He'd always had trouble spending money, even now that he had plenty. He'd grown up with virtually nothing, had worked his way through school by depriving himself of everything except the most basic essentials, but now that he was a partner in his lab practice, he no longer suffered from money troubles. Lauren had been instrumental in getting him to relax about spending. She deprived herself of nothing. She had no patience with being conservative. It was probably healthy, he realized, giving in to impulse every once in a while.

But even so, the price of the necklace made him break out in a sweat.

"What's your return policy?" he asked.

"Thirty days, and keep your receipt." The jeweler sent him a look of incredulity. "What, you think she'll refuse this? You got to be kidding."

Rob shook his head. "I don't know her that well."

"You will after you give her this."

At the very least, Rob reasoned, if Twyla refused the necklace, he could give it to Lauren.

As soon as he had the thought, his head reeled. What was he thinking? You didn't recycle one woman's gift to another. He slapped a bank card on the counter.

The jeweler rang up the sale and couched the ruby necklace in a long black velvet box. Handing it to Rob with the charge slip, he said, "Congratulations. It's going to be a great weekend."

CHAPTER EIGHT

GWEN MCCABE BEAMED at her daughter. "You have no idea how long I've waited for this day," she said. "I thought you'd never get over your disenchantment with men."

"What makes you think I'm over it?" Twyla asked, checking the latch on her overnight bag. It was a wonder she even had an overnight bag—she never went anywhere.

"Well, of course you're over it if you're going to your reunion with that nice young doctor from Denver."

Twyla decided not to burst her mother's bubble. Gwen believed this weekend meant more than it did, and Twyla didn't see the harm in letting her think this was something fun and pleasurable. She privately hoped that her return to Hell Creek would inspire Gwen. Perhaps seeing her daughter take this big step to face the past would help her take a step of her own.

Off the porch.

Twyla shut her eyes briefly. Her mother's panic attacks had grown so severe that Gwen no longer left the house. She made it as far as the top step of the porch, then nearly collapsed from anxiety. Her mother's condition had gone on so long that they seldom spoke of it anymore, because they got nowhere.

"You must be so excited," Gwen continued, oblivious of Twyla's thoughts. "Remember how you used to look forward to your dates when you were in high school?"

"That was high school, Mom."

"Nevertheless, you must feel like you're walking on air."

"I feel like projectile vomiting."

"Oh, Twyla—"

"He's here!" Brian came charging through the house from the kitchen, Shep right behind him, toenails clattering on the scratched wood floor. Twyla had brought him home from school early today, so that she could say goodbye. "Rob's here!" Brian left the house at a run, pausing at the top of the porch steps to leap over them, landing on the battered earth with full symphonic sound.

"Someone's glad to see him, at least," Gwen pointed out.

Brian bounced like a rubber ball, peppering Rob with questions as he led him up to the house. Twyla was, for a moment, entirely captivated by the picture of her small son walking beside a tall man, Brian's worshipful face turned up and Rob's dark head bent low as he listened intently to whatever the boy was saying.

Don't do this, she warned herself. Don't start thinking…But she was already thinking it. Already thinking that no matter how much she loved Brian, no matter how hard she worked to raise him, no matter what she taught him, there was one thing she had never given him—a father. And no matter how many times she'd tried to convince herself Brian was fine without one, she couldn't help thinking that it was important.

Her own childhood was filled with memories of her father. There were certain things a mother couldn't give a child—the bristly feel of a cheek rough with five-o'clock shadow. The belly-deep laughter set off by tasteless jokes that made a mother roll her eyes. The way to punch a baseball mitt down into the palm of your hand. The illicit joy of sneaking downstairs at midnight to eat sandwiches made with peanut butter and marshmallow fluff. The big-shouldered protector who appeared in the doorway to ward off a nightmare.

Many boys had grown up with less, she told herself. Rob Carter was a perfect example. Raised at Lost Springs, he had been deprived of both parents—and look how he turned out.

Just look.

"Hi." She could barely choke out a greeting when he came into the house. The prospect of throwing up was becoming progressively more real.

He gave her a dazzling prime-time TV smile. "All set for the big event?"

"As set as I'm ever going to be, I suppose." She knew it was too late to chicken out, but Lord, she wanted to. Oh, how she wanted to.

He picked up her overnight bag and zippered garment bag. "Is this everything?"

"Yes." She clutched her purse in front of her like a shield, and went down on one knee in front of Brian. "Be good, sport. You do everything your grandma tells you, all right?" She looked deep into her son's face, dreading his reaction. What if he got hysterical over the prospect of her leaving for the weekend?

Then again, what if he didn't?

He didn't. He gave her a big hug and a kiss on the cheek and said, "Bye, Mom. Bye, Rob."

Gwen beamed like a chaperone on prom night. "Don't give us a thought. *The Wizard of Oz* is on TV tonight, and we're making Yellow Dinner for supper."

"Yellow dinner?" Rob asked.

"A family tradition," Twyla said, a little embarrassed.

"Everything yellow," Brian explained. "Corn on the cob, macaroni and cheese, chicken nuggets—"

"Hey, that's almost worth staying for," Rob said.

Gwen laughed. "Don't tease. Just have a Midori on the airplane. You know, that yellow melon liqueur."

"Mom, I don't think this airplane is going to have Midori on board."

"Oh, heavens, I forgot the camera. Don't move—I want a picture of you two flying off on your big adventure."

Twyla stood up with a shudder. The last time—the only time—she had been in a plane, it had been with her father.

And they hadn't been drinking Midori.

"I'VE GOT A LINE on a new crop-dusting formula," her father had shouted over the clatter of the Stearman's radial engine. "As soon as I close this deal to be the exclusive agent in the state, your mom and I'll be on easy street."

She had felt a momentary thrill for him, thinking that perhaps this time his luck would hold. It was pleasant, flying low across the valley scooped out between the Tetons, imagining her life shaping into something that remotely resembled her dreams. "It was nice of you to ask Jake to look over the legal contracts."

"Hey, he's family."

"More than you know, Daddy," she yelled, clutching the sides of the cockpit. "I suppose I should tell Jake first, but I can't help myself—I'm pregnant."

He had crowed with sheer delight, throwing back his head and laughing into the wind.

It was the last day she had seen her father alive.

"READY, TWYLA?" ROB asked. "Smile for the camera." With smooth familiarity, he slid his arm around her.

Shaken by the memory, she took a deep breath, burying the old hurt as best she could. Then she lifted her chin and grinned broadly, blinking in the aftermath of the flash.

"All set," she said, taking the proffered arm of Rob Carter.

They walked out on the porch. At the last second, she spun around and opened her arms. "One more hug and kiss," she insisted, and Brian plowed willingly into her. She felt the warmth of him, smelled the little-boy scent of earth and grass and dog, and a loving ache tugged at her heart. "See you, sport. I love you."

"Love you, Mom. Gotta go help Grammy in the kitchen."

When the screen door slammed behind him, she turned to Rob.

He was staring at her with a fascination that reminded her of a hungry wolf.

"What?" she asked.

He kept staring. "You're a good mother, aren't you?"

"I have no idea. I'm making it up as I go along. So you think I'm a good mother?"

He hesitated. "Yeah. I guess."

Before she could reply, he turned away, picked up her bags and walked to his rental car. She followed, feeling strangely guilty, as if his admission had slammed a door shut between them. He had been raised at Lost Springs, not by a mother. What did he feel, watching her with Brian? She wanted to ask him, but she didn't know how.

She got into the rental car—a Cadillac STS—and looked over at him.

Lord, that profile.

"I guess we should stay away from touchy subjects, huh?" she asked.

He turned to her and propped an elbow on the back of her seat, his scowl melting beneath the charm of a boyish grin. "Not if we're about to become engaged."

"What?"

"Engaged. You know, to be married." With a casual lack of haste, he turned on the car and backed down the rutted driveway.

"I know what engaged means," she said, her fingertips suddenly cold as she folded her hands nervously in her lap. "I don't see what it has to do with us."

"It was Mrs. Spinelli and Mrs. Duckworth's idea. They think we should tell people at your reunion that we're engaged."

"That's absurd."

The Cadillac cornered low and smooth around a curve in Brown's Branch Road. "I know. Maybe that's what I like about it."

"We really don't have to—"

"I know that." He put on his sunglasses. "But we're going to. If I show up as your date, people will think I'm just some Joe Schmo you picked up at random."

"Or picked out of a catalog like a packet of burpless cucumber seeds."

"Yep. Can't have that, can we?"

"I don't see why—" She broke off when he turned west off the Shoshone Highway. "This isn't the way to the county airport."

"We don't leave for two hours."

"So where are we going?"

"Just sit tight and you'll see."

She watched the landscape slip by, a whir of wild-flowers and sage and low scrubby hills rising to the far-off Owl Creek peaks, topped with eternal snow. "This is the way to Lost Springs."

"Uh-huh."

He wasn't much for explanations. Ever since the day of the auction, Twyla had felt strangely disoriented and out of control, and the present moment was no different. But there was something else she felt when she was in the presence of Rob Carter—alive. Her skin and scalp tingled with awareness in the breeze, and a sense of anticipation built in her chest. She felt almost reckless, ready to take chances again. Those were two things she had never felt in her life when it came to men.

Her father had been interesting, certainly. Fascinating, truth be told. But with his freewheeling ways and wild dreams, he had never, ever been safe. Jake, on the other hand, had been safe. Comfortable, predictable and—she should have known this from the start—dull. Perhaps that was why, after the pain of abandonment had dulled, she had never regretted his leaving, hadn't considered contesting the divorce, the papers served to her by a stranger who represented Jake had seemed a fitting conclusion to their relationship.

She decided to enjoy the novelty of feeling interested and reckless all at once. It was a rare man who could inspire that. She relaxed in the passenger seat and watched out the window. Rob drove through the peeled-log gateway of Lost Springs, stopped briefly at the security booth, then continued on to the main campus. He drove slowly to the spreading oak tree where she had hung the raffle quilt. She flushed, remembering the way he had rescued her as she dangled from a branch.

"Now what?" she asked.

He stopped the car in the shade. "Now…it's time you learned something about the man you're about to marry."

CHAPTER NINE

"YOU'RE CARRYING THIS a little too far," Twyla said, her voice huffy with disbelief.

"So you're not interested in where your fiancé came from?"

She hesitated, the skeptical expression on her face softening to...something he didn't want to recognize. But he couldn't help himself. She had the most compassionate heart of anyone he'd ever met. Her wise-cracking exterior was just a facade.

"No," she said quietly. "But I wouldn't mind hearing about you."

Rob got out and went around the car, holding her door open. One of the things the Lost Springs staff had hammered away at was manners. It seemed a small matter to youngsters found abandoned in motel rooms or showing up, abused, at the gates of the ranch, but part of rebuilding the boys' self-respect included preparing them to live their lives, not just survive. They were groomed for every possible social situation, from door opening to fish forks to ballroom dancing. He and the boys who had come through the ranch with him used to snicker about it, but in later years he had been grateful for the lessons.

He hadn't actually concealed his background from Lauren for months—he simply never brought it up. They'd first met at a charity ball for the Denver Children's Hospital, and she had clearly been impressed by his gallant gestures, his style on the dance floor, all courtesy of Lost Springs. It had been sort of fun, letting her think he was the product of some fancy Eastern prep school and Ivy League college.

It had been a lot less fun telling her the truth.

She'd taken it well enough, he supposed. But he would never forget her face when he said, "I don't have any family," in response to her questions. It had been an awkward ride downhill after that. He'd explained about Lost Springs as best he could, but looking into Lauren's beautiful face, he could tell she had no clue about what his past had been like. The idea of the boys ranch was so alien to her imagination that she couldn't conceive of it, except as an excuse for a charity event. He'd found her confusion charming in a way. It was refreshing to know someone with that level of naïveté about abandoned boys and troubled teens.

By contrast, when Twyla stepped out of the car and looked up at him, he could see nothing but interest and understanding in her expression.

What a stupid idea, bringing her here. Insane. What did it matter what she knew of him?

"Show me where you lived," she said, shading her eyes as a work detail of teenage boys armed with yard implements walked past.

"This way." He walked in front of the administration building. The almost-deserted campus felt different than it had the previous Saturday, when everything had been set up for the auction. Then, a carnivallike atmosphere had prevailed. Today, a pervasive emptiness blew like an ill wind through Lost Springs. It was beautiful, well-maintained—founding director James Duncan, Lindsay's father, had seen to that. But it was still an institution, not a home, and on empty afternoons like this, the fact was blatantly apparent. Rob knew it was his imagination, but he felt himself growing smaller and smaller as he approached the long, low building that housed the junior dorm. He was six years old again and terrified, clutching his mother's hand like a lifeline.

She'd had to pry his fingers off her wrist when it was time for her to go.

"Here," he said gruffly, pushing open the door. He stopped to show ID to the house officer, who gave them permission for a quick look.

The smell hit him first. It was the scent of disinfectant and something he could only categorize as "boy." The atmosphere hadn't changed. The never-forgotten odor still hung in the air, filling his lungs with strangeness and, if he breathed it too long, loneliness. A neat row of low beds lined the long wall. Each boy had a small study carrel with high sides for privacy, a roomy locker for his things, and a bookshelf crammed with books and treasures. The arrangement looked almost military but for a few details.

"The quilts are a new touch," he said.

Twyla, who stood in the doorway drinking in the sight, came into the room, passing her hand over one of the beds. "The Quilt Quorum did them a couple of years ago and presented them to Lost Springs. One for each boy. The project lasted for months."

Each one had a different personality. The main fabric was old faded denim for the borders and around each square, but the individual designs—a horse, a cowboy hat, a sheriff's star—varied. The homemade quilts muted the starkness of the big shared room.

"So what do you think?" Twyla asked.

"It...helps." He walked down the center aisle to the

second-to-last bed. "This was where I slept. Right here."

"You think it's the same furniture, same everything?"

"Probably." On impulse, he moved the study carrel away from the wall and looked at the back of it. Precise rows of notched check marks covered the wooden back. "Yep, this is the one."

"You made all those marks?"

Suddenly he wished he hadn't shown her. "Yeah," he admitted. "I did."

"What for?"

"I was counting."

"Counting what?"

"You figure it out." He turned and strode out of the dormitory, not looking back to see if she followed.

She was quiet as he crossed the quadrangle with long strides. He pointed out the senior dorm, where the older boys each had a small room to themselves, the library and music room, the refectory where meals were served, the gym and rec buildings, the paddock and stables.

In each place, he encountered a ghost. The ghost was always the boy he had been, watching hungrily as family members—sometimes a parent, sometimes an aunt or grandparent—returned to Lost Springs to reclaim the boy who waited there for them. Or staring in fascination as an adoptive family arrived to take one of the boys home. Or curling up into a ball on his bunk, pretending it didn't matter that no one ever came for him.

A light touch settled on his arm, startling him. He pushed the memories away to find Twyla resting her fingers on his forearm, her face turned up to his. "This is harder than you thought it would be, isn't it?"

Damn. She understood. Rob hadn't been expecting that. And as he gazed down into those liquid rain-colored eyes, he felt something ease inside him, the un-knotting of a tight coil.

"Yeah," he admitted. "I guess it is."

"Do you want to talk about it?"

He took her hand off his arm. "What's the point?"

"What's the point of any talking? To get something off your chest. To share something. I'm a hairdresser, Rob. It's made me a hell of a listener. Dear Abby with a blow-dryer."

"Ah, just what I need."

"Maybe you do."

In the lobby of the gym, he showed her a couple of trophies he had won for basketball and track and field. She put her palm up to the glass case. "Everyone must have been so proud of you."

"That's why the trophies are here. They mean more to Lost Springs than they ever could to me."

"You lived here for so long."

"Eleven years."

"I didn't realize a boy stayed here that long. I thought it was more…temporary."

"It is, for some. The ones who come because they're in trouble only stay until they show they can stay out of trouble. Same for those with family problems. In my case, my only next-of-kin was my mother. She was broke, strung out. Said she'd be back for me in a few months, so that's why I was never up for adoption. The months stretched out into years."

"And you never saw her again?"

He stared unseeing into the trophy case. "Nope."

"Ever try to find her?"

"Oh, yeah. She died about fifteen years ago, a 'Jane Doe' in Vegas."

"Rob, I'm so sorry."

"Yeah, well, shit happens. And this place was good to me. I can't complain."

"You have every right to complain. I think you probably haven't done enough complaining. The sorrow has to go somewhere."

He had never thought of it in quite those terms. They walked back outside, and the emptiness yawned painfully inside him. Lost Springs was beautiful in its idyllic ranch setting. It was run by loving, caring people. But it wasn't a home.

Rob had never defined *home* for himself. He knew what it wasn't. It wasn't a dorm at a boys ranch. It wasn't the frat house where he'd lived in college or the cramped studio in Dallas where he'd done his residency. It wasn't his condo in Denver, or the gated estate in Wildwood where Lauren had grown up, or the elegant town house where she lived now.

In time, he convinced himself that home was a place that existed only in his mind. A place full of old things, with a kitchen that smelled of baking and windows that opened to let in birdsong. Surfaces cluttered with framed family photos, and a yard with a tree and a swing and maybe a pond—

He shoved the picture of Twyla's place out of his mind and strode across the parking lot to his car.

"Sorry about this," he said as he held the door for her.

"About what?"

"About dragging you along on a bad trip down memory lane."

"I'm glad you brought me. Really."

"Why?"

"Just…because. I like getting to know people, learning about them. Maybe you feel that way about your patients. You're better off for knowing them.''

He leaned his hip against the car. "I don't have that sort of practice.''

She cocked her head, frowning a little. "What do you mean?"

He dug in his pocket for the keys. "I'm a pathologist. I specialize in analyzing abnormal tissue and fluids. My patients come to me in petri dishes and test tubes.''

"And you like it that way?" She spoke quietly, in a voice that said she'd rather listen than talk.

"Works for me. I can see sixty, seventy people a day. Figure out their problem in the lab, then recommend a course of treatment." Rob had chosen the specialty during his fourth-year rotation. Working hands-on with patients was disorderly, messy, imprecise. He didn't know what to say to an anxious mother or a worried wife, didn't know how to offer hope and healing to a dying man.

But in the lab, logic and precision ruled. As a pathologist, he could stem a virus outbreak and his work could affect thousands, while a family practitioner could treat only one patient at a time. He had the power to isolate a problem, find its solution. He'd built a formidable and lucrative practice doing just that, and now there were four partners in his group. And each day, he went home knowing his work had touched the lives of hundreds of patients, not just a handful. He told himself that was the way he wanted things, and every time he got the urge to change his specialty, he talked himself out of it.

He held open the passenger door for her. When they left the ranch, he turned down a pitted dirt side road. "One more stop on the tour.''

She braced herself against the bouncing of the car on the quarter-mile drive. He pulled to a stop in a secluded, wooded area on a bluff overlooking the swift blue flow of Lightning Creek.

"It's beautiful here," she said. "Very private."

"That," he said, glancing at his watch, "is the whole idea. We'd better get to the airport." As he turned the car, he felt her staring at him.

"Nice view," she said, "but what's the significance?"

He made himself look straight ahead, watching the dusty road. "Lovers' Lane," he said casually. "It's where I lost my virginity."

A little gasp escaped her, but he heard the smile in her voice as she said, "You know, I could have gone all day without hearing that."

They drove along in silence for a while, following the Shoshone Highway to the county airport. Finally, Rob said, in all sincerity, "You're a good listener, Twyla."

A smile lit her face. "You think so?"

"Yeah. I definitely think so."

"I'm flattered. I always thought—" She shook her head and watched out the window as they entered the airport and headed for the tiny rental car kiosk.

"Thought what?"

"Never mind."

He got out of the car, retrieving their bags from the trunk, then opened Twyla's door. "Sorry, lady, but you'll have to spill. No fiancée of mine keeps secrets from me."

He didn't know many women who blushed quite as often as Twyla did. It must drive her crazy, trying to be a smart-ass when your face kept giving you away.

"So?" he prompted.

"It's nothing, really. Just that, back when I'd planned on going to school, I always thought I'd go into psychology or social work, some field that would require a lot of listening and problem-solving and people skills." She sent him a self-deprecating grin. "As it turns out, I am in that field. Sort of."

As they boarded the small commuter plane for Jackson, Rob realized he was worried about himself. For a physician, he was having a hell of a time describing his condition. All his life, he had felt an invisible weight pressing on his chest. No one could see it, no one but he knew it was there, always, pressing on him with the tension of failed hopes.

After one conversation with Twyla, the burden felt about one brick lighter.

When they were settled into their seats, he had to smile at her almost childlike curiosity about the plane, the contents of the seat pocket in front of her, the seat belt mechanism and the blinking panel of dials and gizmos visible through the open door to the cockpit.

"You like flying?" he asked.

"I have no idea."

He frowned, not understanding.

She looked out the small oval window and laughed. "I've only flown once before, in an open crop duster with my father. It wasn't quite the same as this."

He sat in stunned silence for a few seconds, letting the news sink in. Air travel was so commonplace he was sure he'd never met anyone who hadn't flown. Finally, he said, "That's something, Twyla. That's really something."

"What you mean is, that's really pathetic." She grew serious. "Rob, I don't think you realize what you're getting into, taking me to this reunion."

The door shut, and the plane taxied toward the runway. "Honey, we've got nothing but time."

She laughed. "I don't think I need to bore you with my small-town hard-luck story."

"Who said I'd be bored?"

The plane gathered speed and, with a lurch, became airborne. Twyla gasped and reflexively grabbed for his hand.

Rob didn't let go for the entire forty-five-minute flight to Jackson.

In that short amount of time, he came to know her with a clarity and understanding that was rare for him. Something about Twyla intrigued and challenged him. She wasn't so different from him in some ways. She dreamed big dreams, but unlike him, circumstances hadn't permitted her to see them through. When she spoke of the past, her pride and ambition shone through. When she talked about her current situation, it was with self-deprecating humor and a strange, touching, square-shouldered stoicism.

"I feel funny, getting all moony-eyed over the past," she said. "I guess it's just that the reunion has dredged up some old things I haven't thought about in a long time."

"Moony-eyed?"

She sniffed. "And how would a college-educated doctor say it?"

He thought for a minute. "Moony-eyed, I guess. But why do I hear such contempt in your voice when you call me a college-educated doctor? Is there any other kind?"

"I hope not." She stared down at their linked hands. "I try hard not to be bitter about my marriage. But the truth is, I'm pretty wary about men."

"Sounds like it, if your friends have resorted to sending you on a forced date."

She smiled thinly. "It's a mercy date, Rob, and we both know it."

"Look." He rubbed his thumb across her knuckles. "It's not a mercy date, it's fun." He grinned mischievously. Changing subjects, he said, "So tell me about flying with your father. Was he into aviation?"

"He was into everything for about fifteen minutes."

"And you say he died suddenly?" Rob felt himself entering alien territory. Her personal life should be off limits, but she'd been so open with him up to now. He wanted to know her even better. "Tell me about it, Twyla."

CHAPTER TEN

TWYLA WAS SAVED by the bell—literally. She had really put her foot in it, bringing up the past, and Jake, and her father, and all that it implied.

Rob Carter's expression changed from friendly and interested to deeply suspicious. She hadn't hidden anything from him, not really, but the fact that she'd made no mention of the way her father had died until there was no turning back was probably a little incriminating.

Fortunately for her, a soft bell dinged and the pilot announced their approach to the airport in Jackson. He also said, in the mildest of terms, that due to reported wind shears in the area, passengers should expect "a little jiggle now and then."

The first "jiggle" left Twyla's stomach somewhere in the vicinity of twenty-thousand feet. The next jiggle left the imprint of her ruby-slippered fingernails in Rob's forearm. The jiggle after that might have severed her tongue, except that she had her teeth clamped together too tightly to move.

Some of the other passengers added sound effects to the flight pattern. Oohs and aahs and little shrieks and snatches of prayer rose above the general cacophony.

Forgive me, Brian, Twyla silently pleaded. Forgive your pathetic mother for coming to this stupid reunion just to prove some stupid point to the stupid town that witnessed her humiliation. She pictured her own headstone: Here Lies Twyla Jean McCabe. Died Young of Having Too Much Pride.

Then, before she knew it, a loud rush of wind drowned out everything else. She plastered herself back against the seat and shut her eyes, waiting for the end.

The plane touched down with a slow-motion bounce, then roared along the runway, finally slowing to a leisurely taxi to the jetway. Twyla couldn't believe it. She'd survived.

And she was deeply embarrassed.

But when she turned to Rob to apologize for being so clingy, she was amazed to see that his face had gone ghost-white. Beads of sweat covered his brow and upper lip. When he saw her looking at him, he cleared his throat uncomfortably.

"Are we having fun yet?" he asked.

Twyla laughed shakily. She used her free hand to pry her fingers off his forearm. "I think I've scarred you for life."

He waved away her concern. "If that's the worst a woman ever does to me, I'll count myself lucky." Before she could question him about that comment, he said, "So here we are. What do you want to do first?"

"Drink my face off," she said.

"I'd be glad to join you." He stood and moved back to let her go in front of him. "Let's check into the lodge. Mrs. Spinelli claims it has a well-stocked bar."

Trying not to wobble on her weak knees, Twyla made her way to the exit. "What lodge?" she asked over her shoulder.

"I have no idea. Something called Laughing Water Lodge." He patted his carry-on bag. "I've got a map and the key right here."

Sugar Spinelli had left no detail untended. From the

moment they'd stepped into the airport lobby and spied a rental car employee holding a placard with Dr. Carter written on it, Twyla had wondered what else Mrs. Spinelli and Mrs. Duckworth had planned.

A twenty-five-minute drive in the rental car—a late-model red Jeep with a roll bar—took them out the winding farm-to-market road that stretched between Jackson and Hell Creek. They turned into a drive indicated only by a discreet stone marker beside a small, fast-moving mountain stream. Swaying willows and silvery aspens lined the pebbled drive.

The lodge itself was a grand old thing, built of thick logs with small-paned windows and angular buttresses under the eaves. Inside was a great room done in a low-key new-West motif. Twyla tried not to gawk as she inspected the river-rock fireplace with the requisite thick pile hearth rug, the overstuffed furniture in subdued forest hues, the enticing library shelves filled with books she'd never read. Two bedrooms, she noted with satisfaction. They were located side by side, but she'd keep the door shut.

The fridge in the kitchen held a cold roasted chicken, an assortment of side dishes and desserts, several bottles of Moët Chandon and fruit and muffins for breakfast. As promised, the bar was nicely stocked.

"We're not in Kansas anymore," Twyla murmured.

"I love rich people," Rob said. "I really do."

"Even meddlesome, matchmaking rich people?"

Expertly popping the top of the Moët, Rob said, "Mrs. Spinelli must really like the way you do her hair."

Twyla flushed, overwhelmed by the intimate setting. It seemed almost criminal to be in this wildly romantic place, with every detail attended to, for the sake of a deception. "You know it's more than hair."

"Yeah, I guess I do. You going to tell me about it?"

"She had a pretty terrible time when she was sick a couple of years ago." Twyla said no more, because it was personal. There was a time when Mrs. Spinelli would only see Twyla on a house call. A radical cancer treatment had caused Sugar to lose most of her hair. Though her prognosis was good, she was miserable, and she looked it. Every other day Twyla visited her, styling a wig to look just right and doing her makeup. But the work was more than cosmetic. Mrs. Spinelli talked, and Twyla listened, and a deep bond formed between them. When Mrs. Spinelli felt up to going out again, she credited Twyla with all the compliments she received on her recovery.

"Let me guess." Rob handed her a flute of champagne. "You helped her through the illness."

They clinked glasses and Twyla took a sip. The champagne bubbles danced deliciously over her tongue with a taste she hadn't experienced in years.

"She claims I was a big help," Twyla said. "Mostly I just did her hair and listened."

They were silent, drinking their champagne. After a while, he said, "You like helping people, don't you?"

"Always have, I suppose." A wistfulness settled over her. "I wish—" She stopped and took another drink of the Moët.

"Wish what?"

She regarded him levelly. "What is it like for you when you have a case you can't cure?"

"Everyone can be helped," he said. "But some can't be cured, if that's what you're asking."

"I think I am. What's it like?"

"Frustrating, demoralizing, and it motivates me to work harder and dig deeper."

"How deep?"

"Until I figure out the problem. Why do you ask?" He winked at her. "Experiencing any strange symptoms?"

"My mother is agoraphobic," she blurted out, her tongue loosened by the champagne. "She never leaves the house."

He gulped the rest of his drink, swallowing hard. With a slow, deliberate movement, he set down his glass. "You're kidding."

"I wouldn't joke about this. She started having panic attacks after my father died. They got worse until…she simply stopped going out. We're…working on it."

She didn't admit that they had been working on it for years, that most of the time lately they simply pretended the problem wasn't there. It was baffling and heartbreaking to her, and it caused deep shame for Gwen. With a familiar, pervasive sadness she pictured her beautiful mother, stitching her museum-quality quilts, never leaving the old, secure house where Twyla had brought her when she'd lost everything else in her life.

"Damn," he said. "I'm sorry, Twyla."

"No, I'm sorry. I didn't mean to unload that on you, but I started to feel so comfortable with you today, Rob. When you showed me around Lost Springs, I felt I really got to know you."

He touched her arm briefly, but it was enough to heat her skin. "Did you get her diagnosed?" he asked. "This sort of disorder responds well to a number of drug therapies."

"Our family physician gave her a referral, but she refuses to follow up on it." She waved her hand impatiently. "I have no right to burden you with my troubles."

"You've got to put that load down somewhere," he said. "I don't mind. Honest."

Dear God, she thought, reveling in the comfort of honest conversation with this man. It would be so damned easy to pretend this growing friendship was real.

"So, about your invitation," he said.

"What invitation?"

"About drinking our faces off."

She laughed. "I think I'm over the desire to do that."

"All right then, dinner. I think we should eat here rather than go out."

"Are you ashamed of being seen with a hairdresser?"

"Very funny. No, we have work to do."

"What kind of work?"

Rummaging in his duffel bag, he took out a yellow legal pad and a pair of pencils and tossed them onto the pine plank table. "On paper, we've got to become the perfect couple."

THEY SWITCHED FROM the Moët to a dry Vouvray to go with their meal. Twyla loved it all, the rosemary-flavored chicken, the exotic chilled salads with noodles and hearts of palm, fresh rolls warmed in the oven. Feeling relaxed, she sipped her wine and fiddled with the pencil.

"Okay," she said, "where do we start?"

"Where do all couples start?"

"First meeting. Where did we meet?"

"A medical convention," he said. "I meet tons of people at medical conventions."

She had a swift and discomfiting image of Rob Carter having a stimulating technical discourse with a beautiful thoracic surgeon or pediatrician, followed by an even more stimulating sexual discourse. "No," she said.

"What would someone like me be doing at a medical convention? Fixing hair?"

"Fine, then how did we meet?"

"Should we go for something exotic, like a scuba-diving rescue in Hawaii, or something simple, like we were introduced by mutual friends?"

"Friends, definitely. We can blame it on Mrs. Spinelli. A party at her house."

"Okay, so when was that?"

He gazed at her across the table, looking mellow and untroubled, disquietingly appealing. "Let's see, we'd better get this straight. We want everyone to know we're doing the right thing, not just acting on a rash animal attraction that will fizzle in a couple of months."

Congratulations, Mrs. Spinelli and Mrs. Duckworth, Twyla thought. You've finally done it. You've finally found one I could fall for.

"Heaven forbid." She chuckled, but at the same time, discomfort twisted through her, because when she looked at Rob Carter, she felt nothing but animal attraction.

"On the other hand, we want to be in the first flush of new love. So much more romantic that way."

"Of course."

"Six months?"

"Perfect." She noted it on the legal pad. "Six months it is. Long enough to know it's the real thing, but recent enough to still be starry-eyed about it."

"Damn, we're good."

They finished the Vouvray and moved on to a bowl of chilled strawberries and snifters of calvados.

"So what are our plans? Do we want to live in the city or country?" he asked.

"Country, definitely. Healthier for the kids."

"Ah, so we want more kids?"

"Don't you?" She took a gulp of the apple liqueur.

"Yeah. I guess. Someday."

She caught herself wondering if he meant it. No, she thought, it was probably another lie to add to their story. "What's our favorite song?" she asked impulsively.

"The theme from *Rollerball?*"

She giggled. "That's not what you said in the bachelor auction brochure. You said 'Misty.'"

"Who's Misty?"

"It's a song. The brochure said it was your favorite." She hummed a few bars.

He shook his head. "Never heard of it."

"So who wrote that profile of you in the brochure?"

He hesitated, refilling their glasses. "A friend. Hey, we should come up with a new favorite. Isn't that what people falling in love do?"

It had been so long, she wasn't sure she could remember. "I think it should be a romantic song."

"Like what?"

At the moment, all that came to mind was "The Rainbow Connection," which was Brian's favorite. "Let's take our chances." She got up from the table and switched on the radio. "Next song that comes on, that'll be our song."

A decidedly country twang wailed from the speakers, and then came the words "Ever since we said 'I do,' there's so many things you don't."

"Lovely," she said, humming along to the outdated ballad. "Let's just hope nobody asks."

They brainstormed a small, private wedding. Honeymoon in Paris. Laughing, feeling easier by the moment, they constructed a fictional relationship that was so romantic and so entertaining that Twyla felt inordinately satisfied by the notes she had made.

"We did it," she said. "We're the perfect couple with the perfect relationship."

"Yeah," he said, but he wasn't looking down at the paper. "Just perfect. Ever had one?"

She laughed, silly with the wine and the nonsense they had created. "Right. A perfect relationship doesn't exist, pal."

He grew pensive, twisting the stem off a strawberry. "You're pretty young to have reached that conclusion." He pushed back from the table. "Come out on the porch, and you can tell me all about it."

Carrying the legal pad, she followed him outside. It was a typical Wyoming summer night, the stars so bright and abundant she felt as if she could reach up and pluck them from the sky like so many wildflowers. "Tell you about what? What's left to tell?"

He took the pad and pencil from her and set them aside. "This isn't for the masquerade. This is for me."

"What's for you?"

"This."

He didn't move fast, but with a straightforward deliberation she found oddly thrilling. He gripped her by the upper arms and pulled her to him, covering her mouth with his.

Dear God, a kiss. She couldn't remember the last time a man had kissed her. And what a kiss. It was everything a kiss should be—sweet, flavored with strawberries and wine, and driven by an underlying passion that she felt surging up through him, creating an answering need in her. She rested her hands on his shoulders and let her mouth soften, open. He felt wonderful beneath her hands, his muscles firm, his skin warm, his mouth… She just wanted to drown in him, drown in the passion. If he was faking his ardor, he was damned good. When he stopped kissing her, she stepped back. Her disbelieving fingers went to her mouth, lightly touching her moist, swollen lips.

"That…wasn't in the notes," she objected weakly.

"I like to ad lib."

"I need to sit down." Walking backward, never taking her eyes off him, she groped behind her and found the Adirondack-style porch swing, sinking back onto it. Get a grip, she told herself. It was only a kiss.

"I think," he said mildly, "it's time you told me just why you were so reluctant to come back here for the reunion."

"And why I had to bring a fake fiancé as a shield?"

Sitting down beside her, he brushed a lock of hair away from her cheek, and she flinched.

"Don't do that," he said.

"Don't do what?"

"Act like you're not used to me touching you."

"But I'm not—"

"We've been together six months," he said, grinning.

Then she got it. "Okay, you're right. I have to act like we do this every day." Every night, she thought.

"Good plan." Very casually, he draped his arm along the back of the porch swing. "I'm all ears, Twyla. Why'd I have to practically hog-tie you to get you back here?"

She felt a jolt of panic and prayed he couldn't see it in her face. How much should she tell him? How much could she trust him? "It's so predictable. None of this would surprise a soap opera fan. Are you sure you want to hear?"

"I insist on it."

The calvados and the darkness gave her courage—or made her foolish enough to trust this stranger with an old, old hurt. "It started with my marriage."

"The one you were too young for."

"Of course. But Jake and I had a plan."

"Jake—your ex-husband."

"Uh-huh. Jake Barnard. He was three years older, going to Northwest College in Powell. He was like a god to me, always had been. Top of the heap. Captain of the football squad. Voted most likely to...everything. All through high school, I made sure I measured up to the standards he'd set."

"You made captain of the football squad?" Rob gave a low whistle.

"I had to settle for head cheerleader, smarty-pants." She felt as if she were speaking about a couple of strangers, so remote were those two people now. "Hell Creek is so small, I guess you could say we lived in a fishbowl, with the whole town watching us. I didn't mind, so long as there was nothing to hide. It looked as if our lives were all set. Nothing could stop us." She was surprised to feel a thickness in her throat. Even after all these years, it still hurt. "We both got into great schools. University of Chicago for me and law school at Northwestern for Jake. The trouble was, only one of us could afford to go at a time while the other one worked."

"Let me guess. You volunteered to work full-time while he went to school."

"It made perfect sense. He was able to take an extra-heavy course load and attend summer school. Within three years, he'd have his law degree. We knew he'd get a terrific position right out of law school, because there was a firm in Jackson just waiting to hire him. Once that happened, then it would be my turn."

"It's a pretty grim commute from Jackson to the University of Chicago."

She remembered how disappointed she'd been, realizing she'd have to give up the chance to attend one of the best schools in the country.

"Change of plans," she said. "I'd be going to Northwest college in Powell. Anyway, I held up my end of the bargain. I cut hair for three years while he went through law school."

She stared at some distant point in the night sky, remembering. "We had such plans. We'd spend three weeks in Paris—it was always my dream to go to Paris—and then when we came back, he'd go to work and I'd get my degree. He landed a six-figure job at a major firm in Jackson, and we bought a house in Hell Creek. Everyone in town figured we were the fulfillment of the American Dream."

It felt good, talking about it after such a long time. She wondered about Rob, though. "Am I boring you?" she asked.

"No way. I have to hear the rest."

"I couldn't wait to get back to my studies. I remember feeling giddy, browsing through the course descriptions in the catalog. When I found out I was pregnant, I knew it would complicate things, but I had no idea my whole world would explode."

"What do you mean, explode?"

Nervously she set the swing in motion with one foot. "You probably already guessed. It's such a cliché. When I told Jake about the baby, he asked for a divorce. Within a few weeks, he went to France with some resort property heiress who went to high school with me. She already had her degree."

"He never contacted you about Brian?"

"No. I guess it's stupid, but I never pursued child support and Jake never offered."

"So whatever became of him?"

"My husband?" Her voice sounded soft, wistful.

"Ex-husband, you mean."

The sharpness of his correction startled her out of a dreamlike reminiscence. "What? Oh, Jake. I haven't seen him since the day I left Hell Creek, right after my father's funeral. He...um...showed up for the ceremony, but I couldn't bring myself to face him. He married the heiress, made a big name for himself in Jackson, ran for Congress, and as far as I know, they lived happily ever after. He never wanted to see Brian. Never calls him."

"So what were you hiding, Twyla? Marriages don't always work out. There's no shame in that. Especially since you were the injured party."

"But—" She took a long breath. The night air was filled with the fresh scent of water from the stream and the peppery perfume of daisies. "It wasn't what you'd call a quiet, discreet divorce. Jake's first case with his law firm was to sue my father over a contract with a crop-dusting chemical company."

Rob said a word that both seared her ears and pretty much summed up her opinion of the whole situation. Then he was quiet for a long time. She didn't know him well enough to guess what he was thinking. She didn't know him well enough to ask.

"So I suppose that's why coming back here didn't appeal to me. I was never fond of circling buzzards." She halted the motion of the swing and looked off into the distance at a swirl of stars. Her pride again. It was always getting in the way. The truth about Jake was that her experience with him had filled her with so much hurt and shame, she knew she'd never recover completely.

How did women get over their divorces? she wondered. Some of them—Sadie, for example—sailed through the trauma, cut their hair, lost weight, took up smoking and came through just fine. Twyla, on the other hand, was sure she'd spend her life wearing a scarlet *V* on her chest—*V* for victim.

What she really wanted was not to care. Not to care that she never had the chance to go to college, to go to Paris, to spread her wings and see where the wind took her.

But she did care. She cared so much that it burned a hole in her heart.

"No," said Rob, setting the swing in motion with his foot.

"No what?" she asked, startled out of her thoughts.

"No, it's not stupid that you never went after your ex for child support. I suppose if you were incapacitated you could make a case for it. But you're not. You're strong and capable, probably more so than your ex ever was."

She turned on her half of the swing so that she was facing him. Shadows fell across his face, but she could tell he was looking at her.

"That's about the best thing anyone's ever said to me."

He laughed. "Clearly you don't get out enough."

The night breeze sneaked across the porch, and she shivered. Quite naturally, without making any sort of production of it, he reached down and pulled her bare feet onto his knee. "Cold feet," he commented, covering her toes with his large, warm hand.

Twyla panicked, though she held herself perfectly motionless. He couldn't have known the alarm that was erupting inside her.

Yet he must have seen something in her face, maybe in her posture. "What's wrong?"

"This wasn't in the script."

"What wasn't in the script?"

"This. The bare feet in your lap," she said with an impatient shake of her head.

"You have beautiful feet." He rubbed them slowly, very slowly.

Thank God for Diep. Diep and her glorious pedicure. She closed her eyes and thought, *You have great hands.* Wild horses couldn't make her say it aloud.

"You think I have great hands, don't you?"

"What makes you say that?" she demanded.

"The way your eyes sort of half close when I do this." He rubbed her foot firmly, his thumb tracing the arch and curving around the shape of her heel.

She yanked her feet out of his lap and stood up, pressing herself against the porch rail. "Look, you don't have to do this."

"Do what?"

"This…this…everything. But especially the foot thing."

"Twyla. Do you have a foot fetish, or does any touching have this effect on you?"

She felt so hot she nearly burst into flames. She stayed in the shadows, hoping he couldn't tell. "It's a forbidden intimacy," she said.

"Forbidden? Isn't that a little melodramatic?"

"It's too personal."

He grinned wickedly. "I think that's the point."

"I think we can get through this weekend without having to make that particular point."

"We're supposed to be having a good time."

"We are having a good time," she insisted.

"Oh. Glad I asked."

She blew out a heavy sigh. "Okay, so we're not. I take full responsibility. We can head home tomorrow and forget this ever happened."

"Not," he said, "on your life."

"Why not?"

"Mrs. Spinelli and Mrs. Duckworth would tar and feather me if I didn't see this through. Besides, I like you, Twyla. This is a great house. We should enjoy it." He got up from the swing, crossed to the railing where she stood. "And you've got to quit shying away from me. I'm not Jake Barnard. No woman put her life on hold in order to pay my way through school." He paused, a devilish grin on his face. "Although, if I'd known that was an option, I might have pursued it."

"Ha. Typical male."

He ran his finger down her bare arm and back up, drawing circles on her shoulder. Until this moment, she'd never known that shivers could feel warm.

"Twyla, calm down and let yourself have fun with this. That's the point. You're spending your first weekend away from your son and your mother and your shop, and if you don't have a good time doing it, then you've betrayed them and yourself."

In spite of herself, she chuckled. "Oh, you're good, Dr. Carter."

"Thanks. Now, get back over to the swing and put your feet in my lap."

The surprising thing wasn't that he came right out and said it. The surprising thing was that she obeyed.

CHAPTER ELEVEN

THE NEXT MORNING, Rob woke up thinking about kissing Twyla. He had to take a cold shower immediately. Lifting his face to the needles of water, he told himself he shouldn't have touched her. But for the first time in his life, he had no willpower where a woman was concerned. No control, no honor, no conscience. And no idea why, of all the women he'd ever met, the one who sent him into a tailspin was a small-town hairdresser.

After his shower, he was tempted to phone Lauren despite the early hour. It was probably best he didn't, because the mood he was in now wouldn't make for a pleasant conversation. "I hope you're satisfied, babe," he'd say. "You told me to do what it takes to show this girl a good time. I'm just following instructions."

He put on a well-worn pair of jeans, a T-shirt and his favorite hat. It was a Red Sox baseball cap, so old Lauren wouldn't even speak to him when he wore it. His cowboy boots were equally lived-in, and he was glad he'd brought them along. He couldn't remember the last time he'd worn them. Years ago he used to practice team roping, a skill he'd learned at Lost Springs. Lately, however, he didn't have time to ride a horse, much less go roping. Lauren's idea of riding was to put an English saddle on some high-strung, overbred Arab mare and try to coax it over jumps.

Before leaving the cabin, he stood outside the door to

Twyla's bedroom. She had left the door slightly ajar, and through it he caught a glimpse of her that nearly sent him back to the shower. She lay in a cloud of covers, her features softened by the morning light through the curtains. Her hair spilled like liquid across the pillow. One bare foot and one bare shoulder were visible. The rest he could only imagine—and did.

Muttering under his breath, he went outside. The cool, sharp morning air gave him a much-needed draught of sanity. The agreement was for a romantic weekend without the romance. How hard could that be?

It was a long hike to the Laughing Water stables, clear on the other side of the meadow, though still in sight of the lodge. He didn't mind the walk, though. He needed time to think. Yesterday had been extraordinary, and too damned fun to dismiss as doing his duty. The talk, the honesty that had come out between them, smack in the middle of plotting their deception, had amazed him.

In one day he had told Twyla McCabe more about himself than he'd ever told anyone. And he'd learned more about her than he had a right to know. It was hard to keep a woman like Twyla at arm's length. He was glad she'd told him about her jerk of a husband and the dreams she believed no longer could come true.

And he was glad he had kissed her.

He had spent half the night tossing and turning, trying to be sorry he'd crossed over the line, but guilt couldn't overshadow the raw pleasure of holding her in his arms.

The scuffed toes of his boots were damp with morning dew when he reached the stables. A young boy was working in the paddock, beating saddle blankets with a crowbar.

"Got a couple of horses we can borrow?" Rob asked.

He squinted through a cloud of blanket dust. "You the folks up at the cabin?"

"That's right." Rob handed him the card he'd found on the table of the lodge. "I thought we'd take advantage of the invitation."

"Sure thing." The youth had a bandy-legged ease around horses that Rob recognized. At Lost Springs they had worked with livestock a lot, riding and roping, and many of the boys went into ranching as a result. "You experienced riders?"

"One of us is." Rob took a wild guess that Twyla didn't ride. She just didn't seem the type.

"We'll give you Mabel and Trapper, then. Mabel's perfect for beginners." He offered a quick overview of the riding trails in the area, mentioning that the sight of a horse on the streets of Hell Creek was as common as a bicycle.

Rob helped him saddle up, handed him a generous tip and mounted Trapper, leading Mabel along by the reins as he returned to the cabin. It felt good to be on a horse again.

When he got back to the cabin, the sun had reached a dazzling midmorning point, raising heat shimmers across the swishing meadows. Twyla sat out on the porch, sipping coffee from a mug and eating a bagel. She wore jeans, a white T-shirt, and red sneakers. Her hair was damp from the shower. An ordinary woman in ordinary clothes, he thought, so why did his heart speed up when he looked at her?

She wasn't his type, he told himself for the thousandth time. His type was a woman who wore designer jewelry and dressed in a long silk peignoir and high heels for breakfast.

But when Twyla saw him and broke into a smile, he forgot all about dressing up for breakfast.

"I don't believe it," she said, setting down her coffee mug. "Do you know how fabulous you look in cowboy boots, leading a pair of horses to my door?"

He grinned, liking her frankness. He had no doubt she would be equally frank if she didn't think he was fabulous. "So mount up, cowgirl. We're going for a ride."

"No way." She finished off the bagel.

He dismounted, tethering the horses to the porch rail. Without giving her a second glance, he grabbed her hand.

She pulled back, resisting him. "I don't ride."

"They say Mabel is the perfect horse for a beginner."

"I'm less than a beginner. I'm an unhatched tadpole. Wild horses couldn't make me get on that horse."

"We've only got tame horses." He gave her hand a squeeze. "How about a little trust here? That's what this is about. Trust. I wouldn't ask you to do anything you can't handle."

She twisted her wrist, extracting her hand from his. "Just because I grew up in Wyoming doesn't mean I know how to ride."

"You don't have to know. Mabel knows what to do."

Twyla eyed the big horse dubiously. "A horse that's smarter than me. I'm so flattered."

He laughed and held out his hand. "I'll work on my manners before tonight."

TWYLA COULDN'T TELL if the swish and swirl of blood in her ears stemmed from terror or excitement. She had gone to bed last night thinking of Rob's kiss, and she'd woken up this morning still dreaming about it.

She'd tried and tried to tell herself it didn't matter, it

meant nothing, they were only faking it, but her heart wouldn't listen. Now she hesitated, studying Rob's face. He didn't laugh often, she realized, and his smile was rare, too. The sight of him laughing and reaching out for her made her skin tingle. It also made her reckless, and like a starstruck teenager, she took his hand.

"All right," she said. "I'm trusting you."

"You won't be sorry." His hand felt large and sturdy as his fingers closed around hers. He brought her over next to the horse and rested his palm at the small of her back.

And just for a moment Twyla fell utterly still. She closed her eyes. Everything inside her seemed to heat and gather at the two places where he was touching her—hand and back. Dear heaven, it was more intense than last night. She had forgotten. She had completely forgotten what it was like to feel a man's touch. She had forgotten the sensation of holding a hand bigger than hers, sensing a protection from things no more scary than everyday living.

Which, when you really thought about it, was the scariest thing of all.

"Hey, you don't have to do this," Rob said.

Without even opening her eyes, she knew his smile was gone. She wanted it back. "Are you kidding? You talked me into it. Now I'm committed." And when she opened her eyes, the smile was back, though tinged at the edges with curiosity.

"I thought I'd lost you for a minute," he said. "You looked a million miles away."

"Oh, I wasn't." She realized she had better get busy or she'd lose her mind, fantasizing about this guy. "Show me what to do, *kimosabe*."

His expression grew warm with approval, and she

knew she had said something to please him. He brought the horse to the steps and positioned her at its side.

"Put your foot in the stirrup." He held it. "Grab the saddle horn, like this, and swing your other leg up and over. I'll help you. Don't worry. I won't let you go."

She prayed the seams of her blue jeans would hold as she fitted her foot into the stirrup. She prayed he wouldn't grunt from the strain as he boosted her by the upper thigh to help her on the horse.

He didn't. The sound that came from him sounded more like a low-throated moan. A sound of pain?

She landed in the saddle with a solid thump and looked down at him. "Are you all right?"

His grin widened. "You have a nice butt, Twyla."

She clutched the saddle horn with both hands, letting her hair fall forward to hide her flushed face. She shouldn't feel flattered by the crude remark, but Lord help her, she did.

Then she realized how she must look with her death grip on the saddle horn and its proximity to her—

She shook her hair out of her face. "Okay, so I'm on. Now what? Oh, God." She made the mistake of looking at the ground. "Holy cow," she whispered.

"What?"

"This horse is three stories high."

He laughed. She was getting used to the pleasant, evocative sound of a man's laughter, though this time it failed to ease her terror. "A horse always looks taller from the perspective of the saddle," he explained.

"The air is too thin up here. I need an oxygen mask. I'm getting vertigo."

"You're fine." He showed her the basics. "Take the reins in your right hand. Mabel's probably used to beginners, so don't worry about making a mistake."

He made a kissing sound with his mouth. Apparently his appeal wasn't limited to the human species, because the horse walked forward. The mare's gait felt clumsy and off balance, and Twyla hung on for dear life.

"Pull this way to turn. See how she feels it on her neck?" He demonstrated left and right. "This'll make her back up."

Twyla stifled a scream as the horse took three giant steps back. She felt as wobbly and vulnerable as a wedding cake bride about to plunge into the champagne punch.

"And this is stop," Rob explained. "Whoa. Say 'whoa.'"

"Whoa, damn it." The horse obeyed. "Get me down," Twyla said. "My life insurance policy is inadequate."

"You'll be fine," he said a second time, swinging himself up into the saddle of the other horse. "Mabel will follow me. I'm irresistible to females."

True. She didn't say it aloud, but as she watched him adjust his funny old baseball hat and noted his easy posture in the saddle, she knew he was right.

"Okay, remember what I told you. We'll take this little trail. The kid at the stables said it's a nice, easy ride." He made a smooching sound with his mouth.

By the time Twyla realized the sound was for the horses, both animals had turned away from the lodge and headed along the poplar-lined path.

Mabel immediately surged ahead of the other horse.

Twyla gave a shriek and clutched the saddle horn. "Hey, you said she'd follow you."

He angled his horse across the path and moved in front of her. "Guess she's got a mind of her own. It's all about control, Twyla. Half the work of riding a horse is here.'' He touched his temple.

"The other half is getting saddle sore already,'' she grumbled.

Yet to her surprise, she found, after a few false starts, that he was right. The connection between her and the mare was primal and governed by the slightest nuance of touch—her legs against the mare's side, her pressure on the reins, even the way she leaned slightly forward. Each movement meant something to the big animal. After a while, she discovered an unexpected and heady satisfaction in being able to control a twelve-hundred-pound horse.

Rob gave her pointers, one at a time so she wouldn't try to remember everything at once. Chin up, heels down, back straight. It all came surprisingly naturally to her. Before long she was able to relax and enjoy the scenery, welcoming the sights after a seven-year absence. The mountains surrounded the valley like a broken-edged bowl, the highest peaks searing white against the blue summer sky. Meadowlarks and red-winged blackbirds swooped across the expanse of wind-stirred wildflowers, and the sun was warm and welcome on her face.

"Like it?'' he asked.

"Yes,'' she said, amazed as the dirt path converged with a larger, tree-lined lane leading to town. "I used to know every blade of grass around here.''

"And now?''

"I guess I still do.''

"So how about giving me a tour?''

Her hand tightened on the reins. She looked out across the vast field of rippling grass, then lifted her gaze to the saw-toothed mountains that rose like a fortress between earth and sky. "I grew up within sight of those mountains. I used to think God lived up there." Chagrined, she admitted, "I went looking for him once, but all I found was a possum and a case of poison ivy."

Lord, Twyla. Keep rambling on. He'll be asleep in no time.

Instead, he watched her with such rapt fascination that she smiled. "You must be a good doctor."

"It wouldn't be right to be a doctor otherwise," he said simply.

"It's none of my business, but I have an observation to make."

"Yeah?"

"You seem to be so good with people. I wonder why you confine your medical practice to a lab."

"I'm not good with people," he said. "Just good with you." As soon as the words were out, he looked away and added hastily, "I mean, I'm not good with sick people, only with their labs. I'm a loner, Twyla. Always have been and probably always will be."

She was afraid to dig deeper. She sensed there was so much more to him than she knew. Each time she saw a new facet of him, she liked him better.

They crossed a fallow pasture that abutted the old Jensen place. Once they cleared the pasture, they'd be on the main street of the town.

"Are you sure you want to do this?" she asked.

"Oh, yeah. A trip down memory lane. It's your turn, Twyla."

He didn't know what he was asking.

"I can't promise you'll find it riveting," she said uncomfortably.

"I didn't ask you to be riveting," he said. "Just honest."

"Why?"

"Because honesty is the only reason to do anything."

What a strange thing to say, she thought. Apprehension spread over her like a heat rash as they drew nearer and nearer to the town. She saw things that tugged her back into the past, awakening memories, like the Munchkins of Oz coming out of hiding.

It was just an ordinary western town, she realized with some surprise, smaller than she remembered, but not quite so drab, either. People went about their business, but she didn't recognize anyone. There was the bridal shop where she had worked, spending every free moment poring over travel brochures, dreaming of the places she would go one day. And there was the Twisted Scissors Salon and Beauty School where she had cheerfully learned her trade because it was a good way to bring money in while Jake went to school.

Then it would be her turn.

She had been unbelievably trusting back then. She was more than making up for that mistake now. She trusted no one—yet she had allowed Rob Carter to coax her onto a horse. That was something, at least.

Each chair in the Twisted Scissors was occupied, but from a distance she couldn't see any faces. Some of the women were probably getting ready for the reunion tonight.

Twyla kept looking around, wondering if a passer-by would recognize her. But the young mothers pushing strollers, the guys on the sidewalk in front of the feed store, and the bank teller smoking a cigarette outside the bank hardly gave her and Rob a second glance.

Funny, she had felt like a bug under a magnifying glass seven years ago when everything had fallen apart. Now she was just some woman passing through.

Hell Creek High School was at the edge of town. An ordinary place of brick and mortar, marred by the scars and scuff marks of teenage exuberance. Shreds of crepe paper draped the entrance to the ball field, and a sign, already fading in the strong sunlight, proclaimed Congratulations 1999 Grads.

She pulled up on the reins, just as Rob had shown her. Mabel lurched to a halt beneath a shade tree, dropped her head and tugged indolently at a clump of grass.

"There it is," she said. "My alma mater." She regarded the concrete footpaths in a wagon-wheel array, the park benches lining the walk. Somewhere her initials were carved in the seat of a bench. TM + JB = 4-EVER. Hard to imagine that she had once believed in forever.

"I recall every detail," she said wonderingly. "The way the hallways smelled of disinfectant, the scratching of chalk on a blackboard, the sound of kids stampeding to the lunchroom, everything." She stared across ten years at the girl she had been. "I thought I was something back then. Really something."

"You were," Rob said. "Still are."

"Oh, yeah." She spoke lightly, but a strange sadness swept through her. She missed that girl, that laughing, eager girl who believed anything was possible and who was limited only by the boundaries of her dreams. There was something magical about holding an unshakable belief in oneself.

She wondered if anyone actually retained that belief long into adulthood. Thinking of her father, she thought, yes. It was possible, but was it wise?

"Seen enough?" she called to Rob.

He sat on his horse some distance away, a far-off expression on his face. She wondered what he saw when he looked at the past. Part of her wished she knew him well enough to ask.

He swung to face her, tipping back his hat. And said the one thing she had been dreading all day. "Show me where you used to live."

CHAPTER TWELVE

TWYLA WANTED TO REFUSE him, but she couldn't. He'd come a long way with her, and she was pretty sure it wasn't because the Hell Creek High School's ten-year reunion sounded like a great time. Besides, for reasons of his own, he had shown her a glimpse of his own past. Walking with him through the cabins and dorms at Lost Springs had taught her more about this man than she could learn from doing his hair for five years. She could only imagine what it had cost him to return to a place full of such bittersweet memories.

With a tug of the reins, she turned Mabel down a tree-lined street. Until today, she'd never understood the appeal of horseback riding, though she'd grown up in a place where it was common. There hadn't been room for a horse at the Lazy Acres Mobile Home Court.

The uncomplaining responsiveness of the horse had a calming effect on her. The unhurried walk allowed the sights to unfold gradually. Somehow, nothing seen from the saddle could intimidate her.

They passed houses where kids she used to envy had lived. The older wooden homes on tree-lined streets had the sort of solid permanence she'd never known.

Jake was going to buy her one of those houses once his career at the Jackson law firm took off. It was one of many promises he'd broken.

At the end of the main road, the shade trees thinned

to weedy, unkempt shrubs, the territory of her youth. A half-empty industrial park with dismantled engines and odd auto parts strewn around marked the edge of town. After that was a surprise. Something new. Unexpected.

"A drive-through funeral parlor?" Rob scratched his head.

"That's what it looks like." She felt a horrified sense of amusement. The place looked as polished and prosperous as a graduate with a new haircut. The area had been professionally landscaped with little hillocks covered in bark mulch and planted with flowering shrubs and small trees. The long, low building was as discreet as a whisper, camouflaged in the landscape with natural earth tones and river-rock walkways. The drive-around had a tinted glass viewing window. She wondered if a sensor was triggered when a car drove over the barrier, turning on the light. Without even getting out of the car, mourners could send condolences via a tube, like making a deposit at the bank.

"You missed your calling, Daddy," she said softly. "You would've made a killing with this." She laughed darkly at her own pun.

"He would have?"

"He owned this piece of property, a hundred acres going back to the riverbank," she explained. "It was repossessed when my father…died." She almost said "was killed," but she didn't want to get into that with Rob. "He tried a little of everything on this lot. One year it was growing jojoba beans because he read somewhere they were the next big boom in farming. Oh, and that thing over at the river's edge is where he was going to put in an emu barn." She pointed to a broken concrete slab in the distance.

"Emus?"

"You know, those big birds with long skinny feathers that look like dreadlocks. He was convinced emu was going to take the place of beef as the 'other red meat,' but he never did sell a one of them. I think he imprinted the first hatchlings. They followed him around like a flock of six-foot ducklings." Seeing Rob's face, she laughed. "I'm not kidding. Eventually he donated them to the Winter Ranch in the Texas Hill Country."

"Your father," he said, "must've been an interesting guy."

"You have no idea. His last project was a miniature golf course with a gold-mining theme. You saw the photo at my house. He spent two years building it. It had a working waterfall and a stream with fake gold nuggets, a lookout tower, and hole number eighteen yelled 'Eureka' when you got the ball in the hole."

"Sounds sort of…weird. But fun."

"Everyone in town used their coupon for a free round. After that, no one came back, and the tourism in Jackson didn't spill over."

With bittersweet remembrance, she regarded the long expanse of meadow and riverside. No trace of her father lingered here, no hint of his humor and pie-in-the-sky dreams or his wacky money-making schemes. Just the real world, rock solid. A drive-through funeral parlor where emus used to roam.

She angled the horse back onto the path and rode on, determined not to make a big deal out of this silly tour. But she felt a taut dread in her chest as they came to the place she had called home for eighteen years.

Lazy Acres Mobile Home Court, the billboard read. It was the same sign that had marked the place years ago. A cartoon cowboy, poorly rendered in peeling paint, grinned out at her. At the bottom of the sign was written Day-Week-Month…

"Forever," she muttered. She and her friends used to joke about it.

"Looks like the whole area's been abandoned," Rob said, scanning the dilapidated trailers and overgrown grass.

"And not a moment too soon." Twyla pointed. "That one was our place."

Rob dismounted and took hold of her reins. "Leg over, and then slide down with your belly against her side."

He made it sound so easy, but her legs dangled in midair and the ground seemed a mile away. Then a pair of strong hands grabbed her by the waist. "Easy now," he said gently. "I've got you."

Considering their position, she couldn't help remembering his comment about her butt, and hoped he couldn't tell she was blushing as her feet touched the ground and she turned to face him. "Thanks," she said. Her legs felt wobbly and strange from being on the horse.

He tethered the horses by a ditch where water ran down from the mountains. The animals dropped their heads to drink. She walked toward a double-wide with moss growing on the roof and greenish mildew streaking the textured aluminum siding. A thick, waxy vine snaked up and over the TV antenna. Several of the windows were broken or missing.

Rob was silent and thoughtful as he followed her to the old place. Beyond the valley rose Lost Horse Mountain. She didn't look at it, but she could still picture the unnatural gouge in its granite side. That image still haunted her. She felt Rob's gaze on her, and it was as if he were seeing her naked.

She dared to edge a little closer to the trailer, finally stepping up on a broken cinder block and cupping her eyes to peer in through a window. Old bug-infested wooden pallets were stacked against a wall, and cobwebby garden tools leaned against the counter. "Looks like it's been turned into a storage shed," she said.

"What's that up over the door?" Rob asked.

Twyla stepped down from the cinder block. She had a vivid memory of presenting the gift to her father—a horseshoe she'd found while walking home through the Barnards' field. She had painstakingly cleaned it and stuck little sprigs of flowers through the nail holes.

"Why, that's just the perfect thing, Twyla Jean," her father had said. "A horseshoe's pure luck. We'll hang it right here over the door and have nothing but good luck from now on. And you hang it in a U-shape so the luck doesn't fall out."

She could hear those words as if he had whispered them into her ear a moment ago rather than years earlier. And they rang with a painful, sad irony. Each new enterprise had pushed her father further and further away from the fulfillment of his dreams. Each failure had dimmed the eager light in his eyes until finally it had been snuffed out entirely.

Twyla didn't realize she was crying until Rob's hand touched her cheek, catching the tear that slipped down it.

"Hey," he said.

She flushed. "Sorry. I was thinking of my father. God, he was a fool and a dreamer, and I loved him so damned much."

He gave her a folded bandanna from his pocket. "All the world loves a dreamer," he said.

"But it's the doer who gets things done," she pointed out, dabbing her face. "You managed to do both."

"Me?" He put his hand to his chest, regarding her incredulously.

"You dreamed it, then you became it." On impulse she stood on tiptoe and unhooked the rusty horseshoe. "You win the prize, Dr. Carter. Congratulations."

He took the horseshoe from her. "Don't be so sure I'm what you think I am."

She tilted her head to one side. "What do you mean?"

"This whole Horatio Alger, underprivileged-orphan-makes-good thing."

"Well, aren't you an underprivileged orphan who made good?"

"Yeah, but—"

"But nothing. You have a right to be proud of your accomplishments."

"Whatever." They walked in silence over to the tethered horses, and he hooked the rusty horseshoe through a loop in his saddle. "So how is it you landed in Lightning Creek, halfway across the state?" he asked.

"Mama and I wanted to make a new start somewhere." She grimaced, remembering the whispers in church, in the grocery store. Everywhere they went, people looked at them funny, said things behind their hands.

That, she realized, had been the start of her mother's problem. Gwen had found it easier to stay home than to go out and face what people said to her. She couldn't take the speculation about the way her husband had died.

"I'd gotten pretty good at doing hair, so I went looking for a salon of my own, working through a business broker. The place in Lightning Creek was up for sale, so off we went. I thought it would be good for Mama, and I guess it was, but she's never really worked through her grief.''

She glossed over the details. She had never told anyone the whole situation. How the town had made a laughingstock of her father over the crop-dusting lawsuit brought against him by his own son-in-law. She'd never revealed his tragic response to the ridicule and his final desperate plan to keep his wife from going broke. How her mother had changed, curling up like a drying leaf and hiding, having to be tranquilized just to get her into the car. How Twyla had fought nausea and morning sickness during the drive across the state.

"It was a pretty tough year, but Mom and I did all right, all things considered." She spoke lightly, determined to prove after the tears that she was fit company once again.

As he helped her back onto her horse, she could not guess at the thoughts behind his eyes. They were interesting eyes, a deep velvet brown that reflected outward—sunshine and summer sky—but kept the person hidden within.

No matter how hard her path had been, she knew his had been infinitely harder. Her mother had problems, but at least she had a mother. It was time, Twyla decided, to tuck the past away and move on.

She smiled, pleased with her resolve, then leaned down and stroked the mare's neck. "I like riding a horse. I never thought I would."

"Then let's try something new on the ride back. I'll show you." He demonstrated how to get the horse up to a trot, then a canter, using heels and knees and that kissing sound, which, she was ashamed to admit, was a turn-on for her.

She found the ride both terrifying and exhilarating. The motion of the horse created an elemental heartbeat rhythm. She could feel its strength, yet there was also a perception of vulnerability, a sense that the horse was essentially a fearful animal with the instinct to flee. The pounding of hooves over earth reverberated upward, and Twyla was startled to feel it in her very center, and the feeling bordered on being unbearably sensual.

Rob rode beside her, watching, occasionally calling out a word of advice or praise for her technique. When they reached the poplar-lined trail leading to Laughing Water Lodge, Twyla let go, feeling a rush of warm summer wind over her skin and through her hair, and she felt like a kid again, carefree, with no more difficult decision to make than what to have for lunch. She knew the state was only temporary, but she loved the idea that the world was taking care of itself without her monitoring it. The horses sped up when they sensed themselves drawing close to home, so the final stretch was a smooth canter. Almost a gallop, Rob told her, impressed by her performance.

At the large stables, she looked around, still seeking a familiar face and half-afraid she'd find one. Most of the workers were too young to know her or were guests at one of the neighboring lodges.

She followed Rob to the main yard, watched him dismount and emulated him as she had earlier, wishing he was there to hold her as he had done before. When her feet hit the ground with a jolt, so did reality—she had rubber legs from all that riding.

Reaching out, she was disappointed to find that Rob's arm wasn't there for her to clutch at. Then she shook her head, half-ashamed of herself. She was starting to want him near her even when she didn't need him. A dangerous turn of events.

"Here, ma'am, let me help you with that." A man in a Shurgood Feed cap and plaid shirt took the reins.

She thanked him, then did a double take. "Willard, is that you? Willard Stokes?"

He stepped away and eyed her, pushing back the visor of his cap. "Hey, Twyla."

She introduced him to Rob. "Willard and I went through school together. It's good to see you, Willard."

"Same here." His grin hardened a little, and his eyes narrowed. "So I guess you're here for the big reunion."

"That's right." She didn't elaborate. She and Rob had cooked up a story, but she wasn't ready to test it yet. And she certainly didn't want to try it out on Willard P. Stokes, who had excelled at rumormongering during their school days.

"So will you be at the Grange Hall tonight?" she asked him.

He looked at her, then at Rob, then back at her again, and a sharp, untrustworthy glee darkened his gaze. Obviously he hadn't changed much in ten years.

"Wouldn't miss it, Twyla. I sure as heck wouldn't miss it. I bet ol' Beverly wouldn't, either."

At the mention of Jake's second wife, Twyla glimpsed the old Willard in his face. The one who had never been able to resist a scandal.

And despite the beating warmth of day, Twyla shivered.

CHAPTER THIRTEEN

SHE HAD FORGOTTEN what it was like to get ready for a date. She had forgotten how nerve-racking and how evocative it really was. A long bath in the deep spa tub left her warm and fragrant, almost lethargic, and she slipped on a thick terry robe provided by the lodge. She applied makeup, using plenty of color, and smoothed lotion on her arms, tinged pink from riding in the sun today. Her hands forgot all their years of experience doing hair, and it took at least six tries to get the French twist just right.

Standing in front of the mirror in her room, she untied the robe and studied herself with a critical eye, something she never did at home.

She looked her age. She had the body of a twenty-eight-year-old mother of one. Which was not the end of the world, she reminded herself. Still, it wasn't quite the same muscular little body that had vaulted into the air at pep rallies, to be caught on one arm by a male cheerleader.

She put on a pair of panty hose priced well into the double-digit range. On their shopping excursion through the Nieman Marcus catalog, Mrs. Spinelli had insisted on the hose, imported from Italy. They were made of pure silk and had a discreet and excruciatingly fashionable diamond pattern.

Once Twyla had them on, she decided they were

worth the splurge. The sheer silk had a peculiar strength that held in things that needed holding in and played up shapes that were still shaped right. She pulled on the tiny red slip, the scarlet silk dress and the ruby slippers. Picking up the red satin evening bag, she looked in the mirror and panicked.

The woman in the mirror was a stranger. She was chic and dangerous-looking, resembling a walk-on in a James Bond film. She didn't look anything like Brian's mom at all. She looked like a…phony.

Of course, that was exactly what she had come here for. To fool people.

She took a deep breath, checked her makeup one last time, and went to find Rob.

He stood waiting on the front porch, and when he turned, the appreciative look on his face made her glad for the forty-dollar panty hose.

"I'm sorry," he said, his face expressionless. "I was waiting for Twyla. Did you happen to see her?"

She burst out laughing. "Amazing what a little makeup and hair spray can do."

"Amazing. That's exactly how you look." He bowed from the waist with mock formality, holding out a single red rosebud he'd plucked from the hedge in front of the lodge.

"You wore the tux," she said, her skin flushing warm with pleasure. She took the rose and caressed the delicate bud with her fingertips. "The one from the bachelor auction brochure."

"Think it's too much?"

"Probably. But who cares? This whole situation is too much. I'll deal with reality tomorrow."

"Good plan." Without warning, his arm came out and

curved around her, fingers draping dangerously low on her hips.

Flustered, she stepped back quickly. "What are you doing?"

"Don't jump when I touch you like that." A wicked intent glinted in his eyes. "You can't keep acting like I'm a stranger, or people will know we're faking it."

She was speechless, tingling shamefully where he had touched her.

Reaching inside his coat, he took out a box. The slender, oblong shape and size were unmistakable—as was the rush of pleasure Twyla felt as he handed it to her. She had absolutely no idea how long it had been since a man had given her a gift.

She allowed herself to rub her thumb over the smooth, hard velvet of the case. There was nothing quite so enticing as a hinged jewelry box with gold lettering.

She glanced up at Rob. Well, almost nothing. With heavy reluctance, she held it out to him. "I can't take this."

"Why not?"

"It's too...too much. A rose is one thing. Jewelry would move us to another level entirely."

"Who says?"

"I say. A woman knows these things. A beautician knows them better than anyone."

"Well." He flipped open the lid of the box, and she had to force herself not to crane her neck to see. "I say I'd look pretty damned silly wearing this myself, since it matches your dress."

He lifted the necklace, and in spite of herself, Twyla couldn't suppress a gasp. The facets of the diamonds and rubies—she prayed they weren't real—caught sparkles of light from the lowering sun. The necklace was extravagant and beautiful, and for one unguarded moment she wanted it with a fierce purity that frightened her with its intensity.

"Honestly, Rob—"

"Hush up, Twyla." With a firm hand he spun her around and looped the necklace around her neck. The coolness of precious metal and stone warmed as soon as it contacted her skin. She felt hypersensitive, every nerve ending reacting to the brush of his fingers at the nape of her neck as he fastened the clasp. When he finished, he turned her around and held her at arm's length.

"Damn," he said, gazing at her throat. "I'm good."

"You are, huh?" Her fingers came up and touched the stones. "You are. And thank you. But I want you to know, when this weekend's over, you're taking this back with you."

"We'll argue about that some other time."

He held the car door open for her, smiling as she got in the passenger side. She smiled back, but inside, she was a wreck. Please God, she thought. Please don't let me like this too much.

Please don't let me like him too much.

Her gaze tracked him as he went around the front of the car. She forced herself to look down at her feet, clicking the ruby slippers together three times. It's not real, she told herself. It's all make believe. At midnight he'll turn into a fry cook at McDonald's. Or his longtime companion will show up. Or he's got his first wife buried in the back yard.

He got in and started toward the main road. "What?" he asked when she turned to him. "You're staring at me."

"Have you ever been married?"

"No. I already told you—"

"Were you and your college roommate close?"

"What—"

"Ever worked in a food service establishment?"

"No. Twyla, what is this about? Why the third degree?"

She flipped down the visor mirror. "Nerves." The fading daylight glinted off the dazzling necklace. It looked even prettier than it felt against her throat.

"Hey, don't be nervous. You faced these people every day for twelve years," he pointed out, annoyingly manlike in his logic. "One more evening won't kill you."

She knew there was some flaw, somewhere, in his reasoning, but she couldn't put her finger on exactly where.

"It's about a ten-minute drive to the Grange Hall," she said. "Maybe we should rehearse our story one more time."

He looked straight ahead at the road, grinning. "It's a great story."

"A lot of fiction is."

"Okay, so where do we start? With the 'Hey, Twyla, what've you been up to?' bit?"

"WHY, TWYLA MCCABE, what have you been up to?"

Rob tried not to laugh when the woman behind the registration table asked the question.

"I've been incredibly busy," Twyla said, hugging the beaming woman across the table. "You look wonderful, Carol. Let's have a drink later and compare notes."

Rob watched her with admiration. She was a natural at meeting and greeting, looking people in the eye with an honest smile. He had no idea why she'd been so apprehensive about coming to this.

Completely at ease, she put her hand lightly on his

arm. "Carol, this is my…fiancé, Rob Carter." Her face glowed with such pride and warmth that it would take a polygraph to know it was false.

He greeted Carol and handed her a credit card. "Robert Carter, M.D.," she said, giving a low whistle.

Twyla's name tag showed her senior picture from the yearbook. She had changed very little, he observed, yet the changes were profound. Naïveté had given way to a womanly maturity that only enhanced her looks.

"So far so good," Twyla whispered as they moved into the main hall. "She's a huge gossip, and she knows everyone."

"Your hand is ice cold," he commented, rubbing her fingers. To her credit, it was the only symptom of nerves. The rest of her—damn, but he liked the color red—the rest of her would make a blind man see again.

And it was funny—her beauty was so extravagant and over-the-top that he never would have pegged her as his type. Normally he was drawn to understated, elegant women who wore neutral colors and didn't show every emotion they had on their faces.

But nothing about this situation was normal, he reminded himself. He was a hired escort and she was a woman with something to prove.

So why did it feel as if something more were going on?

A good-size crowd had gathered in the hall, a huge, creaky place with a high-timbered ceiling. The decor followed an "End of the Eighties" theme with paper lanterns, an open bar and buffet tables lining the walls, tables grouped near the bar area, and a big dance floor. A bored-looking DJ played ten-year-old tunes from his booth on the stage.

Rob played his part with ease, a bland social smile

fixed on his face and his hand resting, with more pleasure than he should be feeling, at the small of Twyla's back. Moving up through the ranks in the Denver medical world had trained him well for this.

They made the rounds, and each time he felt the muscles of her back tense, he gently massaged her there until she relaxed again. People came and went in a blur: The class clown who had become a pharmacist. The disillusioned three-time divorcée. The weary-looking retired teachers. The gay guy and his life mate. The born-again Christian with bleached blond hair and something critical to say about everyone. Photos of kids, homes, pets, and farm equipment changed hands to a chorus of admiring oohs and aahs.

Everyone wore a tag bearing their yearbook picture and a name in bold letters, with maiden names in parentheses. Spouses and dates had a smaller version of the yearbook picture, so people would know who they were with.

Rob observed the proceedings with more interest than he thought he'd feel. He had never been to a reunion before, filing all the invitations to Lightning Creek in the trash. Now he wondered if he should have attended his tenth, just to check in.

These were people who were building their lives. A reunion was a chance for them to compare notes, to check their progress with those who had started out at the same spot. The measuring was as ruthless as Twyla had warned him it would be, and he was glad she had brought him along for support.

"So where are you from?" asked a short, plump woman with kind eyes and a sizable diamond ring. Her name tag read Agnes (Schwed) Early.

"Denver."

"That's nice. I'm so glad for Twyla," Agnes continued. "Everybody wondered—" She let her voice trail off and took a sip of her punch.

Twyla remained deep in conversation with a guy who couldn't keep his eyes off her cleavage.

"Everybody wondered what?" he asked.

"Well, you know. After the way things turned out with her marriage and her father practically on the same day..." She took another nervous sip. "I'm just glad she learned to trust a man again."

The DJ put on an old Dire Straits tune and Agnes smiled apologetically. "If you'll excuse me, I should go dance with my better half."

He was completely intrigued by the hint of Twyla's past. She had told him a lot of things, but she hadn't told him everything.

The music switched to a trendy blues tune. Rob took Twyla's hand. "Sweetheart," he said to her, playing his role of fiancé with ease, "let's dance."

Without apology to the cleavage-gawker, he took her by the hand and led her out to the dance floor. The slow tune enveloped them, and it was no effort to hug her close, to bend and inhale the fragrance of her neck. He had never met a woman so redolent of alluring female scent as Twyla McCabe. She wore perfume, no doubt, but what he smelled was the mysterious alchemy of that scent mingled with Twyla's body.

"How's it going?" he asked, speaking so close to her that when she inadvertently moved her head, his lips grazed her ear. She shivered, and he could feel her quick intake of breath. An answering tightness seized him.

"Sorry." She spoke directly into his ear, as well. "I forgot what you just said."

He shook with laughter and hugged her closer still. He laughed a lot with Twyla. More than he did with—

He choked off the thought. "I was asking you how it's going."

"Oh! Great," she said. "Better than great. This turned out to be a lot easier than I thought it would be."

"You mean you might actually be having a good time?"

She put a hand against his chest and leaned back to look at him. The ruby necklace sparkled in the candlelight. "I am," she said with a smile that outshone the rubies. "I am."

The smile and her words hit him like a blow to the solar plexus. He was in trouble. He was in big trouble. He wanted Twyla. Bad.

The thought must have brought a funny look to his face.

"I guess this must be pretty awful for you," she said sympathetically.

Awful? Falling for Twyla? It was a disaster.

"I get to dance with you." He pulled her closer.

By ten o'clock, she was glowing. The emcee made announcements about who had done what. She read excerpts from the yearbook that made people squirm, and she told long-buried stories about people who had forgotten how foolish they'd been. But it was all in fun.

"And then," Mamie said with a dramatic pause, "there's Twyla McCabe." She fluttered her notes in Twyla's direction.

Beside him, Rob felt her stiffen like a lodgepole pine.

"Long time no see, Twyla!" Mamie called, then consulted her notes. "Let's see, we had French Club. Four years, booster club. Two years, cheerleading. Debate society. National honor society..." She rattled off an impressive list. It was the school career of a top-notch student. Rob glanced at Twyla, hoping to see pride in her face. Instead, he saw a look of regret.

As soon as Mamie moved on to her next victim, he grabbed Twyla by the hand and hurried her outside. Under a whitish blaze of stars and moonlight, he faced her. "So what?" he said, surprised to hear anger in his voice. "So what if you didn't go to college? So what if you don't have some busy, rat-race career? So what if some jerk used you? You've got a great kid and your own business, and you could do a hell of a lot worse than that."

She lowered her head, and he held his breath. Don't cry, damn it, he thought. He just wasn't good with weepers. She'd nearly slain him this morning with her crying. He couldn't take it another time.

When she lifted her face to the light, she was smiling. "You left out one thing."

Rob stifled an explosive sigh of relief. "Without even thinking about it, he drew her close, liking the way she felt next to him. "What's that?"

"I'm marrying a handsome doctor."

The moment froze and crystallized in his mind. Were they still pretending, or was this real? The growing intimacy between them was definitely real, as tangible as the starry sparkle of the ruby necklace around her throat. As substantial as his physical reaction to her nearness.

He eased away from her. "Then you have nothing to worry about, ma'am. Now, can we go get a beer?"

She seemed a lot more relaxed when they went back inside. If anyone had told him he'd actually have fun going to a strange town for a high school reunion, he would have thought they were crazy. Yet after Twyla survived her moment of crisis, she made it fun. He liked the way she put her head back to laugh, the way eyes followed her through the crowded room.

Watching her animated face, Rob felt a rush reminiscent of the feeling he got from nailing a tricky diagnosis. He had made her happy. And it occurred to him that it was a rare thing in his life. It further occurred to him that the way he made Lauren happy was an entirely different process.

"You're a lucky man," someone said.

Dominic Hunt, Rob read on his name tag. "I feel pretty lucky."

"Didn't expect to see her here," Dominic said, rocking back on his heels.

"Why is everyone so surprised to see Twyla?"

Dominic studied his feet. "You don't come back after your father kills himself for the money."

With that one sentence, the world turned to ice. Suddenly things came into sharp focus. If it was true, or if people even thought it was true, then it explained so much about Twyla.

Rob felt as if someone had ripped away a veil and he could see Twyla clearly now—daughter of the town failure. The shame was sunk deep into the center of her. He could only imagine the courage it had taken her to come back.

"She's got nothing to be ashamed of," he snapped.

"'Course not. You can't help who you're related to, can you?"

"Not unless you're related to no one at all."

Dominic frowned, not understanding, and moved on. Rob felt a stab of guilt. They all spoke to him as if he knew the intimate details of her life—as if he had a lover's right to them.

It's none of your business, he told himself as he

crossed the room to rejoin Twyla. She introduced him to a teacher and to the class treasurer, but he barely listened. She offered him another beer, but he shook his head no. What he wanted, whether or not it was wise, was to know just what had happened with her father, why he'd killed himself and why it made her reluctant to return to this town. She clearly had no inkling of his thoughts as she talked to friends and acquaintances, and he couldn't let on that he knew.

His hands were quicker than his brain as they slid to either side of her waist and drew her back against him. She caught her breath but didn't move away. Bending his head—that fragrant neck again—he said, "Feel like dancing some more?"

With cold self-contempt, he knew exactly why he wanted to dance with her. It was the only way he could legitimately touch her. And Lord, he wanted to touch her.

"Excuse us," she said to the teacher and the class treasurer. Then she turned in his arms, smiling up at him. "You're being an awfully good sport about this."

"Am I?"

"Uh-huh. I don't think anyone could ever guess it's a mercy date."

It's not.

He hoped he wouldn't break out into a sweat as he held her in his arms. The song was a vintage tango, the rhythm cool and slow. Twyla swayed against him, a good dancer, having fun in her ruby slippers. Halfway through the song, he lowered his head and whispered to her, "Let's try a dip."

"Right. You have no idea how to do that."

"The hell I don't. Ballroom dancing was a PE requirement at Lost Springs."

"You're kidding."

"Scout's honor. The Duncans were really big on teaching us the social graces. Wanted to prepare us for anything life throws at us. I took dancing between karate and calf roping. So what do you say?"

"You'll drop me on my behind."

"I can't believe you don't trust me. Listen. Here it comes."

"Here what comes?"

"The dip music. It's made for this kind of move. Ready?"

"No."

"Too bad." Rob hoped memory would serve him correctly as the music slid dramatically to a high chord. Holding a forearm against the back of her waist, he planted his foot and leaned swiftly downward.

Startled, she gripped his shoulders and gave a little cry, though no one but him could hear it over the music. But she shouldn't have worried. The move worked out perfectly, and the feel of her in his arms was unexpectedly gratifying. She was laughing by the time he brought her upright and swung her around.

"Very funny, Valentino," she said.

"See? You should have trusted me."

"I should have—" She stopped so suddenly he thought she was choking on something. She stood frozen on the dance floor, her stare fixed at some point over his shoulder, her face a stiff, white mask.

Rob steered her by the elbow to the sidelines. Following her gaze, he spotted a couple he had not seen earlier. They appeared in a dazzle of light from the foyer, a tall man and a slender woman, both of them extravagantly dressed and good-looking. Even before they made it all the way into the room, people flocked around them, hands waving in greeting, mouths smiling and speaking animatedly. The woman's jewelry shimmered with an expensive gleam, and the man's smile was practiced, sharp and sincere.

Twyla watched it all with the stiff-lipped shock he recalled seeing on patients when he had done his emergency medicine rotation.

"Don't tell me," Rob said to her. "Let me guess. Your ex-husband."

CHAPTER FOURTEEN

TWYLA FELT ROB'S HAND pressing protectively against the small of her back, an echo of the way he had held her during the dance. But unlike that moment, when she had felt so vulnerable yet so safe in his arms, Twyla was in a free fall, and no one, not even Dr. Rob Carter, could save her now.

"I thought he was older than you," he said.

"His wife graduated the same year as me."

As she watched the man who had humiliated her seven years ago, she imagined feeling the rush of the wind over her overheated skin as she fell, spinning helplessly out of control. Dear Lord, what had she been thinking, coming here like this? Why had she thought she could survive a confrontation?

"Let's go say hi," Rob suggested, increasing the pressure of his hand.

"No."

"Oh, yeah. We're going to get it over with."

"Let's just leave."

"With our tails between our legs? Sorry, honey. That's not my style."

"But—"

"Mrs. Spinelli's got a small fortune riding on this. And if you don't mind my saying so, the stakes are even higher for you."

He took her by the hand and started across the room.

She thought of pleading with him, turning boneless and sinking to the floor, shouting "fire" to clear the building, but all of those options would create a spectacle, and that was the last thing she needed.

"Please, Rob, please," she said between her teeth. "There's something I haven't told you."

ROB STOPPED WALKING. "Twyla, there's a lot you haven't told me. We barely know each other." And we'd better keep it that way.

He thought about what people had said about her father and grew cold inside. He was a pathologist, not Dr. Joyce Brothers. He had no idea how to deal with people who told him the deepest secrets of their hearts.

"I know all I need to know," he said brusquely, and started walking again, her hand clutched tightly in his. "You can't let yourself be intimidated by some horse's ass."

The man called Jake Barnard was just lifting a drink to his mouth when his wife spotted Twyla. Rob saw Beverly Barnard's hand come up and give a smart tug on Jake's sleeve. Discreetly moving his arm away from his wife, he looked across the room and spied Twyla.

His only reaction was to finish the drink and help himself to another from a passing waiter's tray.

Rob could sense the tension in Twyla, and he suddenly felt cruel, forcing her into a situation she had been at great pains to avoid. But as he approached the square-jawed Jake and his willowy wife, his resolve firmed. Perhaps the meeting would clear away old scar tissue.

A few dozen gazes tracked their progress across the hall. Twyla did an admirable job ignoring them as she walked up to her ex-husband.

"Hello, Jake," she said.

The guy was good at guarding his thoughts, but not that good, Rob observed. The instant he saw Twyla, his eyes nearly popped out of his head. She was a knockout in every sense of the word.

Rob could just imagine what was going through Jake's mind as he stood next to his pale, elegant wife and stared at his vibrant, gorgeous ex. You should have waited around for her, pal, he thought. But he was self-ishly glad Jake had turned to his heiress instead.

"Hey, Twyla," he said, visibly trying to get a grip. "Long time no see."

"Uh-huh." Her smile seemed frozen in place. "Jake Barnard, this is Rob Carter."

"My wife," Jake said, indicating with a nod. "Beverly."

They shook hands all around. Rob noted that Jake had a firm, practiced grip and that Beverly's hand was icy cold.

"We weren't even going to come tonight," she murmured. "But Willard Stokes insisted." Her gaze coasted over Twyla. "Now I know why."

"So let's get all caught up," Jake suggested, leading the way to some benches at the side of the hall. "That's what these things are for, right?" He finished another drink and turned to his wife. "Baby, go get us a few beers, how about it?"

She hesitated, just for a beat, long enough for Rob to read the flicker of alarm in her eyes. Jake appeared to miss it completely as he sat down on a bench, spreading his arms wide in a comfortable, this-is-my-turf pose. Rob waited for Twyla to take a seat, then sat beside her. Beverley arrived with a tray of three beers and a mixed drink for herself.

Jake cracked his open. "A toast."

"To what?" Twyla asked.

"Old acquaintances?"

"New acquaintances," Rob said, and took a long drink. The beer felt cold and biting and incredibly welcome. "To my future with the finest woman in the West," he added, feeling fiercely protective of Twyla.

She made a soft choking sound. Jake didn't seem to notice. "So what've you been up to, Twyla?" he asked. "You look incredible."

She froze in the middle of lifting her beer to her lips. "Do you really want to do this here, Jake? Now?"

He laughed easily. "Guess not. Whatever the lady wants."

Rob took another swig of beer, hoping to cool the fury burning inside him. This guy had abandoned Twyla and his own son. He hadn't even bothered to ask about Brian.

"Why don't you tell us what you've been up to," Twyla suggested. "You were always so good at that."

"Ouch." Jake gave an exaggerated wince. "Sharper than a serpent's tooth, eh, buddy?" He sent Rob a conspiratorial wink.

Rob stared him down. "Sweeter than a rose," he stated.

"Okay, I'm game," Jake said, ignoring Rob's comment. "A few years of lawyering in Jackson. Then I got myself elected to the Congress of the good old U. S. of A."

"Yes, I know."

"Did you vote for me?"

"I don't live in your district."

As they talked, two things became instantly clear. Jake Barnard and his wife drank too much, too fast. And they despised each other. He wasn't sure how he could tell, but the chilling truth lay before him. Perhaps it was in the stiffness of their posture or the cutting quality of the looks and remarks that passed between them. Or in the exhaustion apparent in Beverly's eyes. She was a beautiful woman, but she lacked the expressive face of a woman secure with herself or in a relationship. There was a forced quality to her smiles, a veiled distaste in the way she regarded her husband.

This probably was, Rob deduced, one of those high-profile marriages that had never been founded on love and couldn't withstand the demands of a U.S. congressman's schedule.

He glanced over at Twyla, who seemed fascinated by Jake's account of his first congressional race. Rob had an urge to shake her, to remind her that this was the guy who dumped her after she'd put him through law school. This was the guy who had turned his back on the son he'd never met. This was the guy who had soured her on men so that little old ladies had to force her to go on dates.

"So I hear you're a doctor." Beverly plucked an olive out of her drink, held it between extra-long fingernails, and then ate it. "What sort of doctor are you?"

Funny. She was a martini drinker. Just like—"A pathologist," he said quickly.

"I see."

People never said much once he told them his specialty. After all, what was there to say? "Seen any good abnormal tissues lately?" She leaned back, probably fearful he'd start talking about Legionnaire's disease or *E. coli* outbreaks. People rarely wanted to hear about what he did, which was one reason he liked his specialty. Other doctors were pressed with questions from those hoping for a quick street-corner consultation, but it rarely happened to Rob.

The weird thing was, he didn't mind giving the occasional on-the-spot diagnosis. Didn't mind looking into a person's eyes rather than into a high-powered microscope.

"And you?" he asked, filling the long conversational pause.

"Full-time wife," she said, "which is more work than you might think. The fund-raisers, the parties, the charity auctions." She waved a long-suffering hand and seemed not to notice that his face reddened at the mention of an auction. "It runs me ragged sometimes, so you don't want to hear about it." She punctuated her statement with a deep swig of her drink.

Rob caught himself looking at her shoes. Though he wasn't one to notice a woman's shoes, he noticed these, because only last week, Lauren had bought the same ones. They were fairly ordinary-looking shoes, although they had a little gold thing in the heel that was the mark of an Italian designer. He still wouldn't have noticed, except that Lauren had been unwrapping the parcel while he was there, and the sales slip had fallen out.

Glancing at it, he'd felt his jaw unhinge. The price of those shoes could feed an indigent family for a month. And here were the same shoes, on the feet of a woman who bore an eerie resemblance to Lauren herself. Studying her, Rob got a glimpse of a future he didn't want to see. Everything about this woman was correct—the clothes, the accent, the patina of expensive schooling. Everything that Rob had thought was important, significant, necessary for a successful life. And yet at the heart of it all, there was something essentially unhappy and incomplete about her.

Because she was married to a jerk?

That was probably a large part of it. But at one time, the jerk had been the sort of man Twyla McCabe wanted to marry. So he must have had his brand of charm.

Rob finished his beer, wondering if he was going nuts, analyzing the marriage of strangers he would probably never see again. But deep in his gut lay the uncomfortable realization that he and Lauren were on a path similar to the one Jake and Beverley had taken. The high-profile socializing. The glitzy life. Living in the right place, owning the right things, driving the right car. From the outside, it looked like the American dream. The one he had formulated by reading *Forbes* magazine because he had no family to teach him what really mattered.

Not for the first time, he felt a sick lurch of doubt. What if his idea of having it all was the wrong idea?

TWYLA PUSHED OPEN THE door to the ladies' room and let loose with an explosive sigh of relief. She had made it to the belly of the beast and so far she had survived. Amazing. She had been certain she wouldn't be able to bear coming back here—much less face Jake—without breaking down.

She used the bathroom, then spent a long time at the sink, delving into her impossibly tiny red evening bag for whatever cosmetics she could find.

She glanced up into the mirror and saw the reflection of someone coming in, her arm through the handle of a baby carrier. A discontented mewling sound issued from a mass of pastel-colored blankets. The woman didn't see Twyla at first. She sat down in the lounge area and unbuttoned her blouse.

Twyla snapped her lipstick shut loudly to alert the

woman, then stepped into the lounge area. The woman had one hand on her bra strap. Her face softened into a smile.

"Twyla? Twyla McCabe?"

Twyla studied her, desperate to figure out who she was. But the open blouse obscured the name tag. All she saw was a tired-looking woman with limp brown hair and a thickening body.

"It's me, Darlene Poole." The woman picked up the baby and tucked it into the crook of her arm. "Darlene Poole Lindstrom, and this is Melanie."

Twyla sank to the bench, peering wonderingly at the baby. "Oh, Darlene, of course I remember you." *But you've changed.* "Your baby is adorable. Congratulations."

"Thanks." Darlene gave a dreamy smile and put the fussing baby to her breast. Instant silence pervaded the lounge. Twyla always felt a touch of nostalgia when she saw a newborn. She adored babies. When she first found out she was pregnant, she had envisioned two or three kids. That was before Jake had dumped her.

"Your first?" she asked Darlene.

"Oh, no. Fourth. We weren't even going to come tonight, but at the last minute we decided to get a sitter and drop in for a little while."

"Four kids," Twyla said in admiration. "That's quite a brood."

"Tommy and I left family planning up to Mother Nature, and that's how we ended up with four. He's a rural mail carrier, of all things," Darlene said, fondness softening her smile. "Not quite the milkman, but we kid each other about it."

Darlene and Tommy had been destined for something quite different, Twyla remembered. The drill team leader and the football quarterback. Winningly attractive and filled with enthusiasm, they had gone off to the University of Wyoming together. Twyla had assumed they would wind up with professional careers in a big city somewhere.

While Darlene chatted about her kids, Twyla was quietly amazed at the change in her. From peppy, vivacious cheerleader, she had turned into a decidedly matronly, plain housewife.

Darlene stroked a loving hand over the baby's downy head. "Surprised?" she asked.

"A little," Twyla admitted.

"We had to drop out of college after Thomas—he's number two. We moved back here because my folks gave us the house for a song and moved to Scottsdale to retire. I just got my tomatoes and pole beans in," she said. "Kids and the garden. That's all I have time for."

She finished nursing the baby and changed her with the brisk, efficient movements of a very experienced mother. Twyla felt a momentary pang. She adored Brian with everything that was in her. But she had always dreamed of having more kids.

"But you," she said, placing the drowsy baby in the carrier. "You're more gorgeous than ever, and that guy. Everyone's talking about him. He looks like 007. And I hear he's a doctor."

"We're...very happy," Twyla said, certain Darlene, whose contentment was so genuine, would see through the deception.

But she didn't. Giving Twyla a brief hug, she said, "I'd better go. Tommy wants to get home early. He's taking the boys fishing tomorrow."

Twyla held the door for Darlene and followed her out of the ladies' room. Tom Lindstrom hadn't changed much—he was still handsome and vigorous—yet Twyla noticed a certain aura about him. A maturity.

She couldn't help but smile at the palpable, protective love that radiated from him, from them both, when he took his wife in his arms. With the infant carrier held between them, he slow-danced with Darlene. She closed her eyes and rested her forehead against his shoulder, and a smile of aching sweetness curved her mouth.

None of the big dreams Darlene and Tom had dreamed had come true. But clearly they couldn't be more content. They were absolutely radiant with happiness.

"You all right?" Rob touched her elbow and she turned. She hadn't seen him approach her.

"Fine. But you must be bored stiff by now."

"Your ex is a real barrel of laughs. Let's dance." Without waiting for her to reply, he slid his arm around her and drew her out to the middle of the floor.

Twyla pressed a hand to his shoulder and felt glad for his touch. There was nothing behind it, she realized. He was here to fulfill an obligation—nothing more. Yet the mere sensation of his touch, of his holding her made her feel stronger, more sure of herself.

"So you survived the encounter," Rob said, speaking quietly into her ear. "Lived to tell the tale."

"It appears I did." She looked beyond him, finding Jake by spotting the largest crowd. He had always been popular. That was something that hadn't changed. Yet she no longer regarded him through rose-colored glasses, or with eyes blurred by the tears of hurt.

Based on the brief encounter with him and Beverly, Twyla felt no yearning for that life. No wish to be a part of his world. And fiercely glad that she had Brian and this marvelous night with a great guy.

"Well?" Rob asked. "You want to tell me how it was for you?"

Surprising herself, she said, "It was...not what I expected. Seeing him again didn't upset me the way I thought it might. He's just some guy who wasn't very nice to me once upon a time, and tonight I realized that none of it was my fault."

With startling tenderness, he touched a wisp of her hair, tucking the stray lock behind her ear before he bent to say, "I guess that was worth coming for."

"Uh-huh." Suddenly her mouth was too dry to say more. She wasn't used to talking about such things, not to anyone. She wasn't used to being touched and held, and she liked it so much it embarrassed her.

"You want to get out of here?"

"Uh-huh."

"Back to the lodge?"

"Uh-huh."

"Do you know it's dangerous to be so agreeable all the time?"

She laughed. "Uh-huh."

CHAPTER FIFTEEN

TWYLA FELT HERSELF growing more and more relaxed during the drive home. Strange, because she was fairly certain something would happen when they got back to the private lodge, and the very thought of such a prospect should make her nervous.

But how could she be nervous when she wanted him so much?

How could she be nervous when he had taken her on a journey that had ended with peace and understanding rather than hurtful memories and humiliation?

Undoing his bow tie and opening the collar studs of his shirt, he fell into an enigmatic silence as he drove, and she didn't break in on his thoughts. She didn't want to. Part of his allure was the mystery of him, the fact that she barely knew him, and probably wouldn't ever see him again after this weekend. There was something incredibly liberating in that. Maybe it was shallow, maybe it was silly, and it was definitely improper, but for once in her life she wanted to go wild.

The night had grown brisk from a snow-chilled wind blowing down from the mountains. When they went inside, he took off his tux jacket and made a fire in the huge river-rock fireplace. She took a second bottle of Moët from the refrigerator, opened it and poured two glasses. Sipping her champagne, she stood back, watching him fan the kindling with the bellows until the dry sticks caught and flames curled up around the big yellow larch logs on the iron grate.

"You do that pretty well for a city boy," she said softly.

"What, build a fire?"

She almost said "uh-huh," but she didn't want him to think she'd gone brain dead. "It's definitely a learned skill. I was hopeless with our woodstove the first winter in Lightning Creek. But eventually I got the hang of it."

"We did plenty of camping and orienteering at Lost Springs," he said, using a poker to shove a stray stick of kindling back under the log.

"Ballroom dancing, survival in the wilderness...I think they prepared you for anything."

His gaze flickered over her, and she felt his admiration like a caress. "Just about," he said.

She handed him the champagne and they clinked the rims of their glasses together. "What should we toast to?" she asked.

"Mission accomplished?"

"Was it?"

"You tell me. Did you have a good time at your ten-year reunion, Twyla?"

"Yes. And it's all thanks to you. Cheers." They drank, and she savored the cool, tart bubbles that glided over her tongue and down her throat. She shut her eyes and took another sip. "I should do this more often."

"Do what?" His voice sounded a little strained.

"Drink champagne with a strange man in a remote cabin. It has a certain undeniable appeal to it." She laughed at herself. "I don't think you know how rare it is for me to get away, even for a weekend. To go some-place where I don't have to be somebody's mother or somebody's daughter. It's incredibly liberating."

"Glad to oblige, then." He drained his glass, and Twyla did the same. Holding her gaze with his, he took the glass from her and set it on a side table.

Now, she thought. Please kiss me now before I think up a reason to stop you.

"Good plan," he whispered.

Dear God, she'd spoken the words aloud.

And she wasn't sorry.

It was not a romantic, soft-focus kiss like the one last night. This time it was swift and tasted of harsh need and urgency. His hands felt huge and insistent as they drew her to him, though his mouth was surprisingly soft and supple, pliant lips shaping themselves over hers, imparting the flavor of champagne and something else, something she hadn't tasted in forever but had never quite forgotten. The essence of a man's desire.

The sudden, almost brutal power of his embrace chased off any lingering hesitation she might have had. She might never have a night like this again. She'd be a fool to let it go to waste. So when he finally lifted his mouth from hers, her blood simmered with desire, obliterating reason. "Rob, I have a confession to make," she said.

"Yeah?"

"I was hoping this would happen."

Again, she noticed the hesitation she had seen in him earlier, followed by a reckless growl of animal passion. As he kissed her a second time, his hand deftly unhooked the back of her dress and the zipper slithered downward. With his other hand, he cupped the back of her head, and her upswept hair fell down around her shoulders. She let her head drop back while he kissed her throat, his lips following the circle formed by the necklace he had given her. She felt dizzy, and forced her eyes open before it was too late.

"Um, just a minute," she muttered.

"Sure." He drew back, shoving a hand in his pocket.

She groped for her evening bag, turning back to him with a small plastic packet in her hand and a terribly bright blush on her face. He produced the same item from his pocket, almost at the same time.

"Good plan," he whispered again, and peeled the red dress down her arms.

She reached around behind him and unbuckled his cummerbund, then one by one removed the gold-and-onyx studs of his shirt. A few moments later, Armani's handiwork lay in a heap on the floor along with the scarlet dress. Twyla stood wearing only her national debt panty hose and a tiny red silk slip. She tugged down the waistband of her hose and sent him a bashful smile. "I'm afraid when I take these off, everything will fall down around my ankles."

"Don't worry, I'm a doctor. I'll put you back together again if I need to."

She laughed, flushed with nervousness and need, and discarded the panty hose.

"Everything stayed put," he said, trailing a finger downward from her throat to her cleavage. The finger disappeared into the bodice of the slip, skimming across the tops of her breast and then over, flicking aside the thin satin strap. She nearly gasped aloud but bit her lip instead, hoping he wouldn't guess just how badly she wanted him.

"I wasn't really worried," Rob stated. Then he said no more, lowering his head to put his mouth where his hand had been.

Twyla closed her eyes and tried to inhale the sensations through every pore. This was heaven, she thought, a moment of heaven right here in the middle of her mundane life. She combed her fingers through his hair and down his back, and together they sank down to the thick pile hearth rug. This man was a stranger, yet in some ineffable way he felt familiar. There was something about him that she recognized. Maybe he was something from her own dreams.

She ran her hands up his back again. It had been so long since she had touched a man. She savored the shape and texture of him, long muscular limbs and soft dark hair on his chest, the subtle shadow of whiskers on his cheeks. She wondered how in heaven's name she had lived so long without this. The question of how she would go on without it after he was gone swooped like a cold specter through her mind, but she pushed it away, burned it away with a heated kiss. He pulled off her slip and lifted her so that her breasts brushed his chest, and pure instinct took over. Her hips undulated against his, rising to form a cradle for their joining.

An urgent wildness built inside her, and she clutched at him, her hands and mouth and body begging for him more shamelessly than words ever could. He entered her rapidly, recklessly, and she cried out with the force and the glory of it, and felt the long, rolling waves begin immediately. He brought her to a crest of sensation where she was afraid to move, to breathe, to blink, but just when she thought she couldn't bear to hover there, he took her higher still. It was unprecedented, almost frightening, the level of pleasure he brought her to. She'd had no idea…then she had no thought at all as she tumbled with a cry into ecstatic nothingness, holding him so close against her that she could feel the rhythm of his heartbeat and each silken ripple of his climax.

It was a long time before she could speak, before she could even form a coherent thought. The long, mindless moments had a hazy, surreal quality, punctuated by the indolent snapping of the fire, the subtle flicker of light over their bare legs and hips. Finally, when one of the logs collapsed and sent a shower of sparks up the chimney, she moved, propping one hand on his chest so that she could look into his face.

"Well," she said, hoping she didn't sound as flustered as she felt. "Well. I'm not sure what happens now."

"What do you mean?"

"It's been a long time for me, Rob. A really long time. I don't quite know what to do next."

He had his fingers tangled deeply in her hair. With unhurried deliberation, he freed his hand and let it slide downward over her shoulder, back, hips, thighs, making a silent, wicked suggestion at her most vulnerable spot. "I have a few ideas."

She flushed, feeling a new wave of desire even before the last one had fully ebbed. "Well," she said again, tossing aside the torn plastic packet he had produced earlier, "we've got one condom left."

"Oh, baby." Like a magician, he produced a whole chain of them from his vest pocket. "We've got more than that."

ROB AWAKENED SLOWLY, savoring the syrupy lassitude of a long, untroubled sleep. He enjoyed the feel of a silky-warm female thigh draped over his and the mysterious, exotic perfume of a woman's hair for a full minute before the shock set in.

Holy shit. He had made love to Twyla last night. Not just once, but…he opened one eye and his gaze tracked across the bedroom. They had started downstairs by the fire, then moved upstairs, trailing articles of clothing and champagne glasses and plastic packets in their wake. There had been a bath in the Jacuzzi tub and then on to the bedroom…. God. He had completely lost his mind.

And now he was trapped—in more ways than one. She slept deeply, unmoving, her limbs heavy and relaxed, entwined with his in an intricate pattern. He'd never slept so tangled up with a woman. He'd never held a woman so close all night long.

Not even…damn. Not even Lauren.

Slowly, gingerly, he tried to escape from the soft, warm bed. He lifted the long leg that lay draped over his and set it aside, but even as he did so, he had a flash of memory and found himself thinking about the way they'd made love last night.

She shifted in her sleep. Her legs wrapped around him, holding him close, closer…. He still tried to escape, tried to talk himself out of wanting her. He thought of agar compound. He calculated the mileage his Lincoln Navigator got and pondered the price of beef hides on the commodities market. He tried to think of anything but last night, but her warmth and the scent of her were undeniable, and before he could stop himself, he was hard with wanting her again.

Gritting his teeth, he gently lifted her head from the cradle of his shoulder, easing a pillow beneath the tumble of red curls. She sighed in her sleep, but didn't awaken. When he raised the cover, he got a glimpse of her body. Big mistake. He shouldn't have looked. But damn, she was a goddess.

He managed to slip from the bed. He put on a pair of jeans, nothing more, and left the room on silent, bare feet, going downstairs to make coffee. As it brewed, he stared, mesmerized, then filled his cup and went out onto the front porch. It was high noon and a scorching sun raised heat shimmers over the meadow surrounding the cabin.

Rob sat on the top step, drinking his coffee and contemplating what he had done.

He had lost control, and that wasn't like him. His life was all about being in control, planning things out, going after a goal. He had his lab practice, and the partnership was making him richer than any man had a right to be. He had Lauren, and although they had not specifically discussed marriage, there was a tacit understanding that they would before too long. He lived in Denver, a city with a night life, a trauma center, golf courses, airports, bowling alleys, for God's sake.

What he had done last night put everything at risk. His carefully constructed life. His career path. His relationship with Lauren. He had flung it all away for the sake of a woman with honest eyes and a beautiful body and a compelling way about her that touched his heart.

He finished his coffee and got up, pacing the yard where tufts of grass covered the sun-heated earth. Raking a hand through his hair, he tried to decide how to handle this.

He was supposed to be good at handling things. He usually was. He could look at a problem from all angles, decide what had to be done, then do it.

Maybe he'd get lucky this time. Maybe Twyla just needed that one wild night to get it out of her system. Maybe she'd simply want to get back home and get busy at work and forget all about him. If she didn't want that, he'd find a way to convince her that parting was for the best. That would be the simplest solution. A cordial "Thanks, it's been fun," and they'd go their separate ways.

"Morning," said a voice from behind him.

Startled, he turned to see her coming out on the porch. Her hair was mussed, and she wore a thick, white terry-cloth robe a couple of sizes too big for her. She had her hands shoved into the deep pockets and a smile on her face.

"Morning," he said. And then…nothing. He was supposed to explain the way things were to her, lay it on the line, but…nothing came out, nothing but an answering smile.

"Sleep well?" he heard himself, his traitorous self, ask.

"Couldn't you tell?" She stretched luxuriously, raising her hands above her head and giving him a glimpse of her cleavage. "You?"

"Uh, sure. There's coffee," he added.

"I found it."

"Oh. Good." Furious at himself for not being able to get the words out, he strode up the porch steps. "We've got a two o'clock flight out of here today."

"So we have about two hours to…"

"Yeah, about two hours."

She smiled up at him. "What are we going to do for two hours?"

Something in that smile destroyed the last of his good intentions. "We'll figure something out." He swept her up into his arms and carried her into the house, holding her as if she weighed nothing, a Rhett Butler move he'd never thought himself capable of making. He strode up the stairs with her and laid her ungently on the bed, parting her robe and unzipping his jeans practically in the same movement. Grabbing a condom from the nightstand, he felt her gaze on him, admiring him. No thought crossed his mind as he entered her, only a burning need to have her, to be with her, in her, surrounded by her. And the wonder of it was, she said nothing but seemed to understand. Maybe she didn't realize that it was a sick obsession, that he had no intention of taking this relationship further than he already had, but maybe she didn't care. And for the moment, he didn't care, either.

CHAPTER SIXTEEN

"WHAT TIME IS YOUR flight to Denver tomorrow?" Twyla asked as Rob unloaded her bags from the car.

"Around eleven in the morning," he said, keeping his back to her. The day had gone from bad to worse, he decided. Or, depending on how he looked at it, from good to incredible. Twyla was great. Sex with her was great. But he had to get the hell out of here and back to the real world.

Until Twyla, he thought he and Lauren had an understanding. A solid relationship, one that had a good chance of being permanent. But maybe deep down he was afraid. Maybe he didn't want anything to be permanent, because life hadn't prepared him for that.

Excuses, he told himself. Lame excuses. The truth was, he had no control over himself when it came to Twyla. She was everything he told himself he didn't want, yet she was all he wanted. He had to get away, regain his sanity, reclaim his life in Denver. Lauren would never find out, but even so, everything with Lauren had changed, and the hell of it was, she didn't even know.

He hadn't told Twyla about Lauren. He hadn't seen the point. And after he knew he should come clean with Twyla, it was too late. If he said anything now, she'd be hurt that he'd deceived her. The best thing to do was to get back to Denver and forget this whole thing happened. He hoped Twyla would agree.

They hadn't talked about it on the plane. The flight had been full, and conversations carried weirdly on airplanes, so they had made small talk. A couple of times, she had touched his arm, his leg, quite naturally, as if he were a familiar and comfortable presence.

Why was letting go so damned hard? he asked himself, carrying her bags up to the sorry-ass house she lived in. Why couldn't he just walk away, forget about her?

When he stepped on the top step to the porch, the riser collapsed. Rob dropped the bags and found himself sunk to the thigh in rotten wood.

"Rob!" Twyla rushed to his side. "Did you hurt yourself?"

He shook his head, extracting himself from the gaping hole. "I'm okay. That step's a doozy, though."

Gwen and Brian came to the door. Dinner smells wafted out through the screen. Feeling stupid, Rob brushed off his jeans.

"I'm so sorry," Twyla said, blushing. "I've been meaning to get that step fixed."

He forced a smile. "You've got no choice now." Patting Brian on the shoulder, he said, "Hey, you. I bet you know where I can find some tools."

"You bet, Rob," the kid said, and led him to the shed behind the house.

TWYLA CAUGHT HERSELF chopping basil to the rhythm of Rob's pounding on the porch outside. She smiled, enjoying the sense of busy purpose that the hammering and sawing seemed to lend to the atmosphere around the place.

Then she felt her mother's stare. She could always tell

when her mother was looking at her. She felt a prickle of awareness, and when she looked up, Gwen stood leaning against the kitchen counter, studying her.

"What?" Twyla asked.

"You know what. Spill."

"Mom, I told you everything." Twyla attacked the basil with new vigor, frowning down at the cutting board. "We had a great time, everything went better than I thought it would." She stopped working to enumerate with her fingers as she spoke. "Darlene Poole and Tommy Lindstrom have four kids, Sandra Jaffe's been saved, Harold Fox is an alcoholic, I saw Jake, and the world didn't come to an end."

"That's not everything," Gwen insisted, giving the spaghetti sauce a brisk stir. "You like him, don't you?"

"Sure I like him." She scraped the basil onto a plate of sliced tomatoes, then concentrated on drizzling olive oil over them. "What's not to like? He was a good sport about the whole thing, he impressed the pants off the whole town of Hell Creek, and now he's keeping my son company and fixing my front porch. Can you blame me for liking him?"

"I mean you really like him. In the romantic sense."

Twyla put the plate of sliced tomatoes in the fridge. "Slow down, Mom," she said, even as a warm rush of emotion flowed through her. "I've only known him a couple of days."

"Sometimes a couple of days is all it takes. Especially when you're made for each other."

Twyla thought of the first time she had met Jake. Three years her senior, he'd been in front of her in the lunch line at school and had come up a dollar short. Twyla had lent him the money. He'd promised to pay her back and had asked her out that weekend. She'd been so flattered by his attention, she'd hardly noticed that he never did pay her back that dollar. Odd. It had been a sign, and she'd ignored it. A single dollar might have saved her scads of heartbreak.

She went to the front door to see how the work was coming. Rob and Brian had dragged a pair of sawhorses and a stack of old lumber out of the shed. Rob wore an old baseball cap. Tools that couldn't possibly have been used in decades lay strewn in the yard or dangled from the stiff old tool belt he wore slung around his waist. He handed Brian the end of a tape measure, and with the deep absorption of a pair of brain surgeons, they marked off a plank for sawing. The picture they made, the large man and the small boy working together, caused Twyla's throat to constrict.

Rob finished sawing and took off his baseball cap. Then, saying something to Brian, he peeled off his golf shirt and slung it over the porch rail. Watching him closely, Brian did exactly the same, slinging his Godzilla T-shirt over the rail, as well. It was amazing how perfectly he'd emulated Rob's actions.

"Now, there's a sight we don't see around here too often," Gwen commented, joining her in the vestibule.

Flushed and dry-mouthed from the sight of Rob's muscular, athletic body, Twyla hurried back into the kitchen. "I think I'll make a pitcher of lemonade."

Gwen followed her, fetching a mesh bag of lemons while Twyla got out the wooden hand juicer. "I wonder why the steps waited until today to collapse. I guess everything happens for a reason, even your date this weekend."

"This weekend happened because you Quilt Quorum ladies can't seem to mind your own business."

"It all worked out for the best. You went back home

with your head held high, and got yourself a new beau in the process.''

"Now, wait a minute. No one said anything about a beau." She went to the sink and rinsed her hands, drying them on a tea towel. "I don't want to hear another word about a beau. He's going back to Denver and we won't be seeing each other again."

"Why not?"

"Because that's the way things are, Mom. My life is here. His is there." She took out a sharp knife and started cutting the lemons in half.

"Does it have to be that way?"

Twyla hesitated, setting down the knife. "You tell me, Mom."

Gwen pressed her lips together, her expression pained. "Twyla, I'm so sorry. I'm so ashamed of my—this—illness."

"Mom, it's nothing to be ashamed of." This was a familiar topic, but today Twyla felt more urgency than usual. "You're a beautiful woman. Youthful and full of energy. But if you won't leave the house, life will pass you by."

"We've been over this so many times." Gwen turned a lemon half on the juicer. "Lately Brian's starting to ask why I never go anywhere. I want to get better, but I just panic. Even thinking about it makes me panic."

Twyla felt a lump rise in her throat. Her mother's strange affliction frustrated her, angered her, but mostly it made her sad. What must her mother have been thinking, looking out the window of their trailer that day and seeing her husband crash his plane into the sheer rock face of Lost Horse Mountain? How could Twyla convince her that it was safe to live again?

"Dear God," Gwen said, "it's me, isn't it? I'm the

reason you won't get on with your life, try to find love again—''

"No, Mama, don't be ridiculous."

"And don't you be a martyr to my problems. Tell you what," Gwen said, industriously squeezing more lemon halves with the juicer. "I still have that card your friend Sadie gave me—the one with the number of the anxiety disorder specialist in Casper. And I still have the pills they gave me last time I tried to snap out of it."

Twyla felt a dawning of hope. "Why the sudden change of heart, Mama?"

"Because I saw the way you were looking at Rob Carter just now. And it was the way I used to look at your father."

"And how is that?"

"Like you'd follow him anywhere. I want you to be free to do that, Twyla. Follow a man anywhere."

"That's not freedom," she objected. "I tried that with Jake, and he led me to my own ruin, practically."

"This one is different. You know he is."

They poured the lemon juice with ice and the sugar syrup into a pitcher. "It doesn't matter, Mom. This was a weekend thing. He's out of here tomorrow, and I won't be seeing him again."

While Gwen drained the pasta, Twyla went out on the porch. With a grin of triumph, Brian held something aloft, pinched between his thumb and forefinger. "Mom, look! Rob pulled my loose tooth."

"How about that?" She held out her hand and he dropped the tiny tooth in her palm, then pulled back his lip to show her the gap. "You've never let anyone pull a tooth," she said.

"I used a clean handkerchief," Rob said hastily. His bare chest and shoulders gleamed with sweat.

"It didn't hurt one bit," Brian declared.

She put the tooth in her pocket. Brian wasn't a coward, but he'd never let her get near him, even when a loose tooth was hanging by a thread. He was a different kid with Rob—more confident, more…himself, perhaps. Don't get used to him, Brian, she wanted to warn her son. Don't start needing him.

"You two had better get washed up," she said, chiding herself for wishful thinking. "Supper's ready."

"Man, I could eat a horse," Brian said. He seemed to be making a special effort to deepen his voice. Nothing like a set of tools to raise the testosterone level.

"Show Rob where the powder room is," Twyla said.

"Not the powder room," Brian said impatiently. "The can."

Ducking her head to hide a smile, she went in to get supper on the table.

"ROB," TWYLA SAID, looking across the dining room table at him, "I can't thank you enough for fixing the step."

"It's the least I can do, since I'm the one who put my foot through it." Both Rob and Brian had shown up at the dinner table with hats removed, hair combed and hands washed. He helped himself to a slice of warm bread and added more pasta to his plate. "If this is the thanks I get, I'll stomp holes in the back steps, too. This is delicious."

Both Twyla and Gwen beamed. It was a family trait that they loved to feed people who appreciated being fed. To Twyla's amusement, she saw that Brian kept emulating everything Rob did, from the way he buttered his bread to the way he twirled his spaghetti. Yet even as she hid a furtive smile, she felt a now-familiar tightness in her chest. Her son was growing up without a father. It was not such a rare thing these days, but there was a special energy between a small boy and a man that she couldn't supply, no matter how hard she tried.

Did she want Rob because Brian was smitten with him, or because he made her laugh, or because when they were making love, he made her feel like a goddess? All of the above, she decided.

Her mother was her usual charming self during dinner. Rob listened with polite interest as she chatted on about the Quilt Quorum, the books on Brian's summer reading list, a pro golf tournament she'd seen on TV.

The four of them ate and talked as if they had known one another forever, and there was a delightful ease between them, no strain or awkward tension. Because, she supposed, there were no expectations on either side. On the few occasions she had tried dating, the strain had been there, palpable, because an invisible weight of anticipation pressed on the shoulders of these reluctant suitors. With Rob, no expectations existed. She knew she should take comfort in that, but instead, the thought of it made her unaccountably glum.

Rob took a last swig of lemonade and carried his dessert plate to the sink. "Ladies, I can't thank you enough for the home cooking," he said.

"You already have," Gwen assured him. "Those steps have been a hazard for years." She stood to clear the table. "Brian, I'm going to need help with the dishes tonight."

"Aw, Grammy—"

"And then I'll need help popping the popcorn before the Sunday-night movie."

He dragged a step stool over to the sink.

"Good night, Gwen, Brian," said Rob, taking his hat

from his back pocket. "I'll be back in the morning to finish up."

Twyla followed him outside, down the new steps into the yard. "You're not finished?"

He turned, propping one hip on a sawhorse. His eyes never left her. "Not even close to finished." Then he blinked as if he'd been disoriented. "Actually, the steps are done, but you need a railing."

"I've never had a railing here. I think it fell off before I bought the place."

"Probably violates some building code. I might as well do it right, Twyla, okay? Humor me. I don't get to work with my hands too often."

Everything he said seemed to have a double meaning. Everything reminded her of last night.

"Okay, so we need a railing," she said.

"I'd hate to think of your mom losing her footing."

Twyla hesitated, then lowered her voice and said, "She never comes down the stairs." Catching the expression on his face, she said, "I'm not kidding, Rob."

He held out his hand. "Come here. Walk with me."

It felt good to touch him again, even if it was just holding hands. They headed down the slope to where his car was parked and stood together in the yard, watching the evening breeze stir the tire swing in the big oak tree.

"I know what you're probably thinking about my mother," Twyla said. "Everyone considers her a charming, bright lady, a good talker and a clear thinker. That's why her agoraphobia is so strange, and so devastating. Everyone thinks that surely she's not the sort of person who could be afflicted with some weird psychosis."

"That's more or less what I was thinking," he admitted. "I did a psych rotation in med school. Anxiety disorders are pretty common, and your mother fits the profile. You probably know more about this than I do at this point, but I want you to know, it's treatable."

"I know that. So does Mom." She shivered as the breeze drifted over her bare arms.

"Cold?"

"No, not really." She strolled over to the swing and sat down. "Mom keeps saying she wants to seek treatment. She has some pills from our family practitioner, but I can't force her to take them."

Over at the house, a light came on in the window. In the gathering darkness, the place didn't look so bad. You couldn't see the peeling paint and warped boards. It appeared cozy and inviting. No one would ever guess that for Gwen McCabe, it was a prison.

"Maybe one reason this problem has gone on so long is that Mom is so rational, so grounded that her illness doesn't seem real," Twyla continued. Other than Sadie, Rob was the only person she'd ever felt like discussing this with.

"At first everyone simply called her a homebody. People came to see her rather than vice versa, and they phoned her. There didn't seem to be anything strange about a middle-aged woman who stuck close to home. Sometimes I wonder if I inadvertently contributed to the problem."

"What do you mean by that?"

"I expected her to be there for Brian while I worked at the salon. It's been the ideal arrangement. I've always been grateful to her for staying home, supporting me, having supper on the table after a long day. I praised her for being so available, the model grandma. It's no joke that I'm the envy of the town's working mothers because of Mom."

She touched her foot to the ground to set the swing

into slow motion. "Home cooking, homebody, stay-at-home mom, homemaker. The messages are everywhere, ever notice that?"

"Not really."

"Me neither, until it became clear Mom had this problem. But society promotes the idea. It's considered virtuous for a woman to stay home. On some level, Mom took this to the extreme. Now it's gone on so long, I don't know if she can jolt herself out of it."

She kept the swing in motion, and somewhere in the distance, an owl hooted. "Whew," she said. "And you thought this was going to be your day of rest."

"What do you mean?"

"First you had to fix the porch, and now you're having to be my therapist. I'm not usually such a wreck, honest."

"You're not a wreck." He took a step toward her. "And you're not finished. You never explained how this problem started."

Twyla bit her lip, but she knew she'd tell him. He was so easy to talk to. She had never known a man whose silent, solid presence she could trust, yet she trusted Rob. "It started when my father died."

The words hung in the air for a moment, and he said nothing, seeming to sense that she had to say more. "The lawsuit—the one Jake's firm brought against him—wasn't going well. Dad had borrowed way beyond his limit, and the only things he had of value were a policy on his crop duster and his life insurance."

"Aw, damn, Twyla—"

When he spoke those words, she knew he'd figured out the truth. She stared at the ground, her chest tight with a grief that, at moments like this, felt as fresh and sharp as the day of his death.

"I don't think he really meant to be so dramatic about it. He knew he was headed for bankruptcy because of the lawsuit. He saw a way to leave Mom with something before they took it all away." She swallowed hard, trying to collect her thoughts. "What he didn't realize is that he was all she needed. Not success or money or fine things."

She looked into Rob's face. "How could he have been so stupid?"

"Um, men get that way sometimes."

She nodded, not about to disagree with him. "My father probably never even thought about the fact that Mom could see Lost Horse Mountain from the little window over her kitchen sink. She saw the accident, standing there, doing the breakfast dishes. I can't imagine what that was like for her, watching him crash into the mountain while she's washing his coffee cup."

He took hold of the swing to stop its motion, then cradled her face between his hands. "Twyla, honey, I'm so sorry."

"It was pretty awful, but it was ruled an accident, which is what he planned, I think. There's a scar on the side of Lost Horse Mountain that marks his passing. The policy settled his debts and gave Mom and me a way to get out of Hell Creek."

She felt his thumb skim over the ridge of her cheekbone, catching a tear and brushing it aside. "Thank God we were able to leave. Because everyone knew it was no accident. The talk was making me crazy."

"That's the real reason you didn't want to go back, isn't it?"

"It's the main reason. But it's been a long time. People found something else to talk about, and I managed to quit feeling responsible for everything that happened." She reached up and took his hands from her face, holding them in hers. "I never thanked you for what you did. For taking me to the reunion, pretending I'd actually found some big important doctor to marry me. It meant a lot to me, Rob. Really."

"Twyla, I said I wasn't finished—"

"I know, we need a stair rail." She took her hands from his and stood, walking toward his car. "Can you finish in time for your flight tomorrow?"

"Reilly's opens early. I'll need to pick up some things, and then I'll be out here around eight."

"I'm afraid I'll already be at the salon. I like to get in early for the book work, and on Monday I do volunteer work. Brian'll be at school—it's the last week before summer vacation." She managed to smile. "Mom'll be here, though. You can count on that."

She stopped at the driver's door of the car. This was the best way to say goodbye, she told herself. Lingering and trying to make things last would simply prolong the inevitable. She rose up on tiptoe and kissed his cheek, keeping it brief even though she wanted to press her skin against his, to inhale that scent of expensive after-shave and honest sweat, to touch her lips to his— No. Time to step back into the real world.

"Thanks again, Rob," she said, her voice quavering only the slightest bit.

When she tried to move away from the car, he blocked her, his arm coming up and planting itself against the roof. "Twyla," he said, "about last night..."

She put two fingers gently against his mouth. "Hey, last night can mean...whatever you want it to mean."

"Why don't you ask me?"

Because I'm afraid to hear the answer.

"I don't think you've decided yet."

"Have you?" he asked.

She thought for a moment. "Nope. But when I figure it out, you'll be the first to know." She took a firm grip on his arm and moved it out of the way. "I'd better go inside, Rob. Good night. And thanks again."

She could feel his eyes on her as she walked toward the house, but she didn't turn. She wondered if he knew she lied. She knew exactly what last night meant to her.

Now she just had to think up what she was going to say to Mrs. Duckworth and Mrs. Spinelli.

CHAPTER SEVENTEEN

ROB TOLD HIMSELF he should know better, but after checking into the Starlite Motel, he headed straight for the Grill instead of phoning Lauren right away. A light fog of smoke layered the upper atmosphere of the old place, and attendance was sparse. He guessed that Sunday nights were not terribly busy at the Roadkill Grill.

He ordered a beer and had a seat at the bar, trying not to feel like some poor schmo in a country-and-western tune. He pretended great interest in the White Sox game on the flickering TV on a shelf above the bar, and barely noticed when someone slipped onto the stool beside him.

"Hey, Romeo. So how did the big weekend go?"

He turned to Stanley Fish, who sported a sunburn and a few days' growth of beard. "Off the record?" Rob asked.

"Aw, c'mon. Don't do this to me. I need a scoop."

"Sorry, pal. There is no scoop, period. I went to this woman's reunion, everybody thought she turned out great, and tomorrow I'm out of here."

"So why're you sitting in a bar crying in your beer?"

Rob rolled his eyes. "I'm watching the game."

"You look as if you just lost your best friend. I can't help but wonder why."

"The Sox. They're having a lousy season."

"Right." Stanley ordered a beer and a handful of

darts for the English-pub-style dart board at the far end of the bar. "Up for a game?" he asked.

"Maybe later."

Rob contemplated his life in Denver. He had a perfect woman and a lucrative job to go home to. He could forget about his plane ticket, drive all night and be there by morning. He should do it. There was nothing left for him here. Fixing the porch at Twyla's house was just an excuse to hang around longer than he should.

It was nuts, completely nuts. His life was set. He'd had everything planned out from the time he was sixteen years old. He'd always been determined to make good. Determined to fill the hole left in his life the day his mother had walked away. To him, that meant marrying well, choosing someone stable and reliable, career-minded, popular. Someone like Lauren DeVane. She was everything he'd ever wanted in a woman—stylish, sophisticated, educated and polished.

But she wasn't cute, fun and loving. She didn't listen with her whole heart.

She wasn't anything like Twyla McCabe.

Glumly, he took a sip of his beer. Twyla and her loopy mother and Brian were everything Rob had spent his whole life trying to forget and escape. Small-town working-class people with everyday struggles and plans that never amounted to more than daydreams. Spending time with Twyla had made him take another look around, and he knew his view was shallow.

Against his will, against all good sense, against the central core of his life's plan, he felt drawn to her. Drawn to this woman who grew up in a trailer park, nurtured on the grandiose dreams of her reckless father. This woman who dyed hair for a living. This woman who loved her son and mother so much she'd given up her own dreams for them.

He kept trying to focus on Lauren and their plans and his future in Denver, but his heart tugged him in another direction—toward Twyla and the life he'd always been so determined to escape.

With quick, angry movements he drained his beer and went over to the dartboard, grabbing a handful of darts.

Stanley Fish stepped aside. "Change your mind?"

"Yeah," said Rob, aiming the first dart. "I need to stab something."

THAT NIGHT HE SLEPT poorly at the Starlite Motel in a room that smelled of ancient cigarette smoke and commercially laundered sheets. The flickering neon marquis outside threw a bluish glow between gaps in the drapes, adding a weird strobelike effect. Rob tried not to think, but the beer and dart games had failed him. Alert and restless, he didn't do much more than doze off and on all night.

A couple of times he got up, even took out a road map and calculated the driving distance to Denver. Three hundred miles, maybe. He could have breakfast with Lauren.

But around 2:00 a.m. he folded up the road map. If he did that, he'd forever be haunted by Twyla and her broken-down house. Fixing the porch was something he had to do. There was probably an explanation in one of her many psychology books. The repair would give him some sort of closure so he could move on.

Right. And the moon was made of green cheese.

THE TOWN OF LIGHTNING Creek stirred to life early. Rob showered and shaved, dressing in a T-shirt and the old jeans Lauren wouldn't let him wear in public. He stopped in at the Grill for a cup of coffee. By the time he saw who was in the booth next to him, it was too late to hide.

"Hey, Mrs. Duckworth," he said, his smile both forced and casual. "Mrs. Spinelli."

"Robert, we were hoping we'd run into you here," Mrs. Duckworth said, carefully measuring a spoonful of sugar for her coffee.

"We want a report on the weekend," Mrs. Spinelli said. "We want to know every detail."

He nearly choked on a gulp of coffee. "It went fine, just fine," he blurted out, trying not to stumble over the words. They regarded him as if they had X-ray vision, seeing that he had made love to Twyla…again and again.

"I did everything you told me to do," he said, hoping they'd settle for that. "Took her horseback riding, gave her a present, acted like her fiancé at the reunion."

"Was she the most beautiful woman there?"

"By far." He didn't even have to think about that one.

Mrs. Duckworth clasped her hands. "Oh, perfect. It sounds like Twyla got just what we wanted for her."

And then some, Rob thought.

"So now what?" Mrs. Spinelli asked. "You're going to want to see her again, aren't you?"

"Well, actually, I, uh, I live in Denver, so it'd be sort of difficult," he said, fumbling for words.

"You'll have to come up on weekends, then," Mrs. Duckworth said briskly.

Damn, thought Rob. These two wouldn't give up. They were industrial-strength fairy godmothers.

"Ma'am," he said, "Twyla McCabe is a wonderful woman."

"We knew you'd think so."

"But the weekend's over. We both live separate lives. We don't plan on seeing each other again."

"Nonsense," Mrs. Spinelli said breezily. "You have to understand, Robert. We chose you. Not one of the other bachelors. You. Because we knew you would be the one."

Rummaging in their purses, the ladies paid their tab and prepared to leave. As they stood, Mrs. Spinelli gave him a guileless smile. "We admit to shameless matchmaking, but the next step is up to you."

Mrs. Duckworth fixed him with her steely-eyed stare. "A word to the wise, Robert," she said. "Twyla McCabe means the world to us. Don't break her heart." She closed her pocketbook with a decisive snap. "You always were a gifted student. You won't blow it this time."

He sat there, speechless, while his coffee got cold. They were batty, those two. Truly batty.

At Reilly's store, he bought half a pound of finishing nails, a new saw blade to replace the rusty one he'd used yesterday, some treated pine balusters and a handrail, and a can of wood preservative.

He stopped in the motel office to check out. The desk clerk handed him a receipt and a folded pink slip. "You had a message yesterday, Dr. Carter."

He glanced at the slip. The message was from Lauren. Seeing her name chilled him. "Change of plans," the message read. "Let's meet at the Fremonts' place in Chugwater. Meet my flight in Casper—4:00 p.m."

The fishing place was about a two hours' drive south

of Casper. Maybe in two hours he'd think up what he was going to say to her.

"Looks like you're off to do a little carpentry," the clerk said, peering curiously at the Cadillac. The car looked odd with red-flagged lumber sticking out of its half-closed trunk.

"A few repairs around the old McCabe place."

"You must be a man of many talents."

"Not nearly enough," he said, getting into the car. "Not nearly enough."

GWEN MCCABE GREETED HIM with a cup of hot coffee and a sticky bun that made him roll his eyes in ecstasy. "This could change my religion," he said.

"I was just aiming to get that hungry look off your face."

He wolfed down another one. "Come out on the porch and keep me company, Gwen."

She hesitated, then picked up an oval-shaped hoop with a big quilt square stretched across it. "All right. I'll work on quilting this section."

He watched her closely, noting a slight tremor in her hand when she opened the screen door. She slid the painted wooden chair as close to the wall as it would go and took her sewing in her lap. Rob worked fast, sawing and hammering, making sure everything fit just right.

"You're very good at that," Gwen said.

"I like working with my hands," he told her. "Haven't done it since wood-shop training at Lost Springs."

"We're very lucky you remember the lessons you learned there." Gwen slipped on a pair of reading glasses and started sewing. "It's a pity you missed Twyla and Brian," she remarked. "They always get an early start on weekdays because of school."

Rob didn't look up from the length of wood he was measuring. "We said our goodbyes yesterday."

"You showed her a good time, Rob. I'm grateful to you for that."

Still he didn't look up, though he felt his ears redden. He wondered how much Twyla had told her mother. "A class reunion wasn't quite what I had in mind when I signed up for this bachelor auction thing, but I guess it worked out okay."

"I know it did. Going back to Hell Creek was a big step for her. Makes me think I should be taking some steps of my own."

Rob stopped working for a moment. He felt a bead of sweat trickle down his throat, disappearing into the T-shirt. "Yeah?"

Unlike Rob, Gwen didn't stop working or look up from her quilt hoop. "Twyla said she told you what happened back there."

"She did. I'm so sorry, Gwen."

Her hands sped up, sewing fast. "And she told you what it did to me."

"Yeah."

"I know what it's called. I think I even know what I might do about it—the medication, the counseling. I've read dozens of books and articles on agoraphobia. So has Twyla. It's just a question of deciding it's got to be done."

"What's stopping you from making that decision, Gwen?"

"Ah. That's the big question. The one I ask myself with every stitch I take. I'll find the answer one of these days. The trouble is, one of these days might be years away."

At last she stopped sewing and eyed him over the top

of her narrow glasses. "Did you ever put off making a decision or taking a step because you have no idea what comes next?"

"I always know what comes next. I'm big on planning."

"But if you didn't know. Would you have trouble making up your mind about something?" She stabbed her needle into the fabric again, outlining a colorful fan shape. "I think that's what my problem is. Life with my husband was so uncertain, so unstable, that I never knew what was going to happen from one moment to the next, but he swept me along, and I allowed it because I loved him and he made it seem all right. But then when he was gone, I froze. There was no one to sweep me along anymore."

"And you can't sweep yourself along?"

"Maybe." She poked her needle through the quilt square. "Maybe. But it hasn't happened yet."

Rob worked in silence for a while, feeling an unaccountable kinship with this intelligent, caring and confused lady. When he had done his psych rotation in school, he'd dismissed it as a specialty because, in most cases, doctor and patient reached an impasse, a wall, and couldn't hurdle it. He didn't want that sort of frustration.

Yet sometimes the wall had a door in it. "Gwen, have you ever thought—"

Just then the phone rang, startling them. With an apologetic smile, she went inside and answered. A moment later she stepped out on the porch, her face pinched and white. "It's Brian's school," she said, pressing the receiver to her chest. "He's been hurt."

CHAPTER EIGHTEEN

"Is TWYLA WITH HIM?" Rob estimated the beauty shop was a few blocks from Lander Elementary, so she could get there in no time.

"That's the problem," said Gwen. "Today's her hospital volunteer day. The school can't reach her."

Rob ripped off his tool belt and tossed it aside, already digging in his jeans pocket for car keys. "What happened?"

"He fell from the monkey bars," Gwen said. "It's probably nothing, but the school nurse is a little worried about the bump on his head. Mostly, he's scared and wants to come home."

"Fine." Amazed at the pounding of his own heart, Rob turned toward his car. "I'll bring him home."

"Rob," Gwen called from the porch, "wait."

"What?"

"You can't go get him."

"Why the hell not?"

"You're not authorized to pick him up from school. They won't release him to you."

He stopped walking. All this parenthood stuff was new territory, but he could understand why a school would be cautious. "Are you authorized, Gwen?"

She pressed her back against the screen door. "Yes, but I can't—"

"Damn it, Gwen, that's not an option at the moment. You just said the school won't release him to me."

"But—"

"The kid needs you." Rob told himself getting angry wouldn't accomplish anything. Sucking air between his gritted teeth, he approached the house and planted his foot on the bottom step. "Here, take my hand. We'll go together."

Her hands clutched the phone receiver like a lifeline. They were beautiful hands, strong and shaped by a lifetime of women's work. Cooking and sewing hands, mothering hands.

"Put the phone down, Gwen, and let's go."

Her grip tightened. Then, even as she made a small sound of protest, she set the cordless receiver on the chair arm.

"Brian's waiting," Rob reminded her. "You said he was scared. I'm only sweeping you away."

The color faded from her cheeks as she edged toward him. The terror in her face wrenched his heart, but he forced himself to keep his hand held out to her. "It's okay," he said softly. "It's just a few steps. Keep thinking of Brian."

She clenched her fists tightly at her sides. He could hear her breathing lightly, quickly.

"Do it for Brian," Rob said. "You can do it, Gwen."

She met his eyes, and hers were filled with unreasoning terror. Rob was tempted to simply grab her, carry her bodily to the car, but he resisted. She had to take this step, and she had to do it on her own.

Finally, with a quick, jerky movement, she took hold of his hand. Her fingers were icy cold, gripping hard. He sensed that it was best to say nothing as she took the first step off the porch. She came down the stairs slowly, then stopped as her feet touched the ground. She stared down for a moment, then looked at Rob. "Let's go."

He helped her into the car, hearing the quickness of her breathing as he sped toward town. "Breathe slowly, Gwen," he said. "Long, slow breaths, and think about Brian. He's waiting for us."

She sat quietly, her ashen face moist with sweat, her hands folded tightly in her lap.

"You're doing great," he said, and kept up a stream of encouraging words during the short ride to town. "Brian's going to be glad to see you."

"H-he'll probably think that bump on the head is giving him hallucinations," she said. "In his entire life, he's never seen me leave the house."

"Then this will mean the world to him."

Slowly, cautiously, she turned her head toward him. "It means the world to me."

IT WAS EERIE, walking the halls of Lander Elementary again. The corridors, which had seemed endlessly long to Rob as a boy, now seemed unexpectedly short. The water fountains he'd had to stand on tiptoe to reach were impossibly low. The office, which used to seem intimidating and glaringly lit, was a cheery place that smelled of coffee and library paste.

Gwen walked straight to the counter and said, "We've come for Brian McCabe. I think he's in the nurse's office."

The secretary looked up from her computer terminal. "I'll need to get your name."

"I'm Mrs. Gwen McCabe, his grandmother, and this is Dr. Robert Carter. He's…a family friend." Her voice gathered strength with each word she spoke. "I'm listed on his authorization card."

"Of course. The school clinic is through there."

Rob even remembered the nurse's office, the mysterious hieroglyphics of the vision-screening chart, the paper-covered cots, the immaculate glass apothecary jars of swabs and Band-Aids. He'd been a regular customer here years ago, because he'd worked as hard at sports as he had at everything else in school, frantic to prove he was as good as any kid who went home to a real family at the end of the day. He'd been in a few times to get cleaned up after a playground fight. Every once in a while a boy used to make the mistake of saying something about the boys of Lost Springs, and Rob had to set him straight.

The nurse herself had changed considerably. She had short orange hair, almost-black lipstick, a long row of studs in each ear, and a button on her lab jacket that read No Whining. Gwen's eyes widened a little, but then she focused on Brian, who lay on one of the cots, a blue gel cold pack on his head.

"Grammy!" he said, and Rob figured the look on the kid's face let Gwen know her effort was well worth it.

"Hey, kiddo." She knelt down beside him. "The nurse says you took a spill."

Rob pointed to the lighted scope in the nurse's pocket. "I'm Dr. Carter, from Denver. May I?"

She handed it to him. Rob took a minute to wash his hands at the sink, then went to Brian. "I just want to take a peek at your eyes," he said, moving the cold pack aside. The hematoma on his head was a good-sized one, but the pupils were reactive, his coloring good. Rob couldn't remember the last time he'd laid hands on a patient. It felt strangely gratifying to feel the living warmth of the boy, even during this brief, cursory exam. Not for the first time, he wondered what it would be like to practice outside the lab. Messy, yes, and unpredictable, but the connection was vital. He could feel it in his bones—and in the settled breathing of the small boy on the cot.

"He's going to be fine," he told Gwen, "but we should watch him today, keep him quiet."

She signed a release form. Then she went to Brian, and hand in hand, they left the school. Rob walked behind them, unexpectedly pierced by tender feelings for the boy. He had never given much thought to being a father. What was it like? Suddenly he wanted to know. He wanted it bad.

"Thanks for coming, Grammy," Brian said, getting into the back seat.

"I'm glad you're okay."

As Rob pulled away from the school, he glanced in the rearview mirror. His heart sank when he saw Brian's chin trembling.

"What's wrong?" he asked.

"I want my mom."

"It's her volunteer day at the hospital," Gwen said.

"I want to see her." Brian's voice quavered.

Rob's shoulders tensed. You couldn't reason with a kid who'd hurt himself, a kid who was on the brink of tears because he wanted his mother. "Where's the hospital, Gwen?"

"Out on the Shoshone Highway, about twelve miles toward Casper."

"Can you handle it, Gwen?"

She hesitated. "All right. Yes, let's go."

He turned back toward the highway. "Does your mom like surprises, Brian?"

"I don't think so."

Rob grinned into the rearview mirror. "She'll like this one."

Twyla POSITIONED a white neckroll pillow behind Mrs. Ulrich. "How's that?" she asked.

"Fine, dear," the old lady said. "I'm very comfortable now."

"Ready for your comb-out?"

"Oh, yes, indeed. My son's coming all the way from Des Moines to see me."

Twyla set her box of beauty supplies on the swivel table by the hospital bed. "We'll have you looking pretty as a picture." Sunshine streamed in through the slatted blinds of the small hospital room, bringing a welcome flood of natural light. Working slowly and gently, she unwound the curlers she'd put in an hour before. There was, she'd always thought, a peculiar intimacy in doing people's hair. Touching the head of a stranger was not an everyday occurrence for most people, for it connoted a level of familiarity that usually only existed among family members. But her role made it permissible. Maybe that was why people tended to tell their hairdressers everything.

A person's hair had a certain sacredness about it. In all the years of being a beautician, she had seen the entire range of reactions from delight to despair. The way a woman's hair looked could determine the way she faced the world that day, and Twyla took her job seriously.

Her volunteer work at the county hospital had begun with Sugar Spinelli's illness several years back. Few women, Twyla had learned, were too sick to worry about their hair, and Mrs. Spinelli was no exception. Twyla had lovingly tended her locks until they became hopelessly thin wisps, decimated by chemotherapy. Then they'd turned to turbans and wigs, having more fun than they should in the middle of a grave illness. Mrs. Spinelli always swore the laughter they'd shared had been part of her healing.

So every Monday, after an hour of bookkeeping at the salon, Twyla spent four hours doing shampoos and sets for the patients who wanted them. Mrs. Ulrich, bedridden with a broken hip, wanted to look her best for her son's visit. Humming to herself, Twyla brushed out the baby-fine, silvery locks, arranging the curls artfully, spritzing them in place.

She was glad to stay busy today, because it kept her from thinking about Rob Carter. He'd probably be finished with the porch by now and be on his way to the county airport. She wouldn't be seeing him again. That was the nature of their arrangement. One encounter, an obligation fulfilled, and then it was over. That was what she'd expected, and that was what she'd gotten.

The one thing she hadn't counted on was falling for him.

"Try not to overdo the spritzer, dear," Mrs. Ulrich said gently.

"Oh." Twyla realized she'd pumped a third of the contents on one spot. "Sorry, I'm a little scattered today."

"Busy weekend?"

Twyla winced at the irony. In the space of two days she had returned to the town she'd fled in shame seven years before, confronted the ex-husband who had dumped her, come to terms with her father's death, had wildly romantic sex and—she finally admitted to herself—fallen in love. "You have no idea," she murmured.

"It's good to keep busy," Mrs. Ulrich commented.

"It's never been a problem for me. Almost finished now."

Mrs. Ulrich picked up a hand mirror and peered at herself. "Oh, my, that's lovely," she said. "I feel better already. Honestly I do."

Twyla gave the arrangement a few final pats.

Though the door to the hospital room was open, a light knock sounded. Twyla looked up, shocked to see Brian and Rob standing there, hand in hand, watching her work.

"Hey, Mom," Brian said.

"Hey yourself."

"Mom!" Brian said. "I fell off the monkey bars and Rob says I can stay home the rest of the day even though it's probably just a bump and I'm totally okay. Can I, Mom? Huh? Can I?"

"He's all right?" she asked Rob urgently. Her heart pounded—and not just from concern for Brian. It was the sight of the two of them together that stirred her, frightened her with how fiercely she wanted them both in her life. She scooped the curlers into her kit. "Would you excuse me, Mrs. Ulrich?"

"Of course, dear. I'm not going anywhere." She picked up the novel she had been reading.

"Brian's fine," Rob assured her. "Aren't you, pal?"

"You bet! And, Mom, guess what else?"

Twyla stepped out of the room. She nodded slowly, but she barely heard him. Barely saw him, though the image of him, hand in hand with Rob Carter, would forever be branded on her heart. Yet even this, astonishing and moving as it was, could not compete with the sight that held her spellbound in the too-bright hospital corridor.

Her mouth moved, trying to shape her disbelief into words, but no sound came out. Then, finally, a thin exclamation.

"Mama?"

Pallid, a curl of white hair dropping over her brow, Gwen held out both hands, palms up.

"Surprise," she said softly.

Twyla crossed the distance between them, hugging her mother close. The familiar scent of laundry and talcum powder surrounded her, and Twyla didn't want to let go. She was afraid the moment would disappear, burst like a bubble. Yet her mother felt as solid and real as the tile floor beneath her feet.

Gradually she came to trust the moment and pulled back, keeping hold of her mother's hands. She tried to control her trembling. But she couldn't. Her mother had left the house. After seven years, her mother had left the house.

"You did it," Twyla said, so filled with amazement and joy that she could hardly speak. "You did it, Mama. It's wonderful."

"Yes," Gwen said. "It is."

Slipping her arm around her mother's waist, she walked toward Rob and Brian. "Why now, Mama? What made you decide to come out now?"

Gwen smiled, a sparkle of her old mischief twinkling in her eye. "Maybe," she said, watching Rob's face, "I was just waiting for someone to fix the porch steps."

CHAPTER NINETEEN

TWYLA RESTED HER HAND on the new rail of the porch steps. It felt sturdy and smelled of freshly milled wood. "It's perfect, Dr. Carter," she said with mock formality. "But what about your flight back to Denver?"

He busied himself picking up tools, and didn't look at her. "Change of plans. I'm meeting someone at the airport in Casper this afternoon."

"Well," she said, rubbing the sanded wood surface. "How can I thank you?"

"By putting a coat of paint on it before winter. It's treated lumber, but it'll last longer with exterior paint."

She tilted back her head, regarding the house with a critical eye. The faded shutters and weathered siding depressed her. "The whole place could use a coat of paint. Maybe I'll have it done this summer if the shop revenues are good."

He loaded the last of the tools into an old wooden bulb crate, cleaning up the work site with the precision of a drill sergeant.

She caught herself wondering what he was really like in what she thought of as his "other" life. His real life. What sort of music did he like? What was his favorite food? Did he live in a house or an apartment? There was so much she didn't know, so much she wanted to learn but wouldn't let herself ask.

He should have been gone by now, and part of her

wished he was, because knowing she'd have to say goodbye to him was torture. Even so, the extra hours he had stayed due to Brian's mishap had been an unexpected bonus.

Or maybe the universe was trying to tell her something.

Gales of boyish laughter drifted on the wind, and they both looked up at the top of the slope where Gwen and Brian were picking berries. Elation clutched at Twyla's heart. "She's never picked berries with him before," she confessed. "He always picked them alone, or with me, and then brought them to her for sorting."

Rob set down the toolbox and studied Brian and Gwen thoughtfully for a moment. "Everything's more fun with a partner." He seemed embarrassed for having said so, and added a stray nail or two to the box. "I hope your mother's on the road to recovery."

"This is the biggest stride she's ever made. I don't think she'll turn back now. I'm going to ask her to see her doctor again about the counseling and medication." She stopped even pretending to stay cool and turned to him, pressing herself against the stout railing he had built. "That's what I can't thank you for, Rob. For Mom."

"Twyla, I didn't—"

"You did." Somehow she knew he would try to duck away from taking credit for this. "In seven years, no one could get her to leave this house. Seven years, Rob."

"She took that step for Brian, not me. He needed her. When the school called, she had no choice."

"The school's called before, once or twice. She always found a way, a perfectly sane and logical way, to get around going. Today she could have phoned Mrs.

Duckworth. She's on the call list for emergencies. But she didn't. It's a huge stride, Rob. I thought you doctors were into taking credit for miracles."

He laughed and picked up the box. "I'm not that kind of doctor."

"Well, maybe you ought to be."

"What makes you say that?"

She tried not to stare at his arms, muscles bunched with the weight of the large wooden crate. "A hunch. It's hard to imagine you in a lab all day, growing bacteria and looking things up in books."

"Actually, I spend more time in consultation with other doctors and researchers and lab techs. When I look something up, I tend to use a computer." He carried the toolbox toward the shed.

"All right," she said, following him. "But it's still not the same as seeing patients." She wasn't sure why she felt so adamant about this. He had an important job. His work saved lives. Yet she couldn't help wondering what the job gave him.

"True. There are lots of different kinds of doctors. Most people are only aware of the ones on the front lines." He disappeared into the cobwebby dimness of the shed.

"So you don't like working with people?" she asked from the doorway.

"Not like you do. I saw the way you were working with that patient at the hospital."

"Mrs. Ulrich?" She smiled fondly. "I did her hair, that's all. She wanted help getting ready for her son's visit from Des Moines."

"It was more than that, Twyla."

They walked together back to the steps. She felt the urge to take his hand—it seemed the most natural thing in the world to do—but she resisted, tucking her hand into her pocket for safety. She took a seat on the porch steps, leaning against the railing.

"What do you mean, it was more than that?"

"The things you do at the hospital—fixing some woman's hair, bringing her a lipstick, whatever makes her feel better. That's the essence of healing. It's something I haven't thought about in a long time. I should thank you for reminding me what's important and making me remember why I do what I do."

"Your field—pathology—is important," she reminded him.

"It's easy to lose sight of the human side of medicine when you're looking at both slides and films all day. You reminded me of that—the human side."

She felt both pleased and embarrassed by his praise. It was a simple thing, sitting on the porch steps and talking with a man about things that were important. Yet in her life, moments like this weren't merely rare but unheard-of. It was frightening how much she liked sharing her thoughts with Rob Carter, how much his attention meant to her. Frightening, because it had to end.

With a hollow feeling in the pit of her stomach, she glanced at her watch, then stood up.

"Didn't you say you were supposed to meet someone at the Casper airport?" she asked.

He hardly blinked. "Yeah. I guess I did." He stacked one sawhorse on top of the other and carried them to the shed.

The weekend was over. The reunion was over. The porch was fixed. Dear Lord, her mother was fixed. Dr. Fix-It had blasted like a whirlwind into her world, rearranging everything. Her life, her house, her priorities.

Her heart.

She felt the moment drawing to a close. She wanted to stop everything, to step back and gaze at each moment of the past weekend like a painting in a museum, beautifully lit and roped off from the rest of her life by red velvet cords. It was something that rare, that special.

She wanted to remember the slant of the sun over the mountains and the sound of Brian's laughter drifting from a distance, the ripple of a breeze across the grassy slope of the yard, the lift of her mother's apron as she walked along the ridge with her face tilted toward the light.

Most of all, Twyla wanted to remember Rob, who had given her so much more than moral support for her journey home. When she had first met him, she had thought he was intimidatingly handsome, unapproachable. Now she found him startlingly accessible, a man she could trust with every secret she had.

He had been the perfect one-night stand, except that she wanted him for more than one night.

Her breath came in short, nervous puffs because she knew what she had to say. She had to tell him...more than thanks. She had to tell him he had changed her, that because of him she felt herself changing, reaching, becoming someone she never thought she would be again and almost didn't recognize.

Someone who could love again.

"So," he said, coming out of the shed, "I guess—"

"Rob."

The urgent note in her voice must have caught at him, because he stood stock-still for a minute, then took off his hat, running a bandanna over his sweaty brow. "Yeah?"

Lord. Being sweaty only added to his sex appeal.

"I wanted you to know...about this weekend..."

"Yeah?" he asked again, clearly intrigued now.

"I feel—oh, God, this is so hard." Just say it, Twyla. Say you don't want it to end, that you're wondering when you can see him again. She got up and paced the yard, hands stuck in the pockets of her skirt. "This weekend was a big deal for me, Rob."

"Good. That's exactly what Mrs. Duckworth and Mrs Spinelli intended."

"No, I'm not talking about that. I honestly don't think their scheme included us winding up in bed."

His eyelids lowered a notch, and she felt a forbidden spasm of remembered pleasure at that hooded look. "That was a bonus, I guess."

She tried to smile, but it wouldn't form. "I can't joke about this, Rob. Remember last night, when you asked me if I'd thought about what...being with you could mean?"

His gaze shifted from side to side. Her earnestness was making him nervous. She plunged onward, anyway. "What happened meant more to me than a one-night stand. So I was wondering what it meant to you."

He fiddled with his watch, though he didn't look at it. She felt guilty, delaying him, but she had to know his thoughts on this.

When he caught her staring at his hands, he sat on the steps and rested his wrists easily on his knees, linking his fingers. "To be honest, Twyla, I didn't want to have anything to do with this weekend, or the whole bachelor auction thing, for that matter. I felt obligated to Lost Springs. When I met you and the quilt ladies, I felt obligated all over again."

"The quilt ladies are sometimes known as the 'guilt' ladies," she said.

Standing up with a restless movement, he propped his

hip against the new railing, testing its strength. "At some point, everything changed. I started to like what we were doing. I liked being with you." The hooded, sexy look shadowed his face again. "I liked making love to you." Then he took a deep breath that expanded his chest, and suddenly there was nothing sexy at all in his expression. "And I shouldn't have."

Twyla folded her arms across her middle, bracing herself. Now she started to sweat, and she felt sure she didn't look nearly so attractive as Rob. She couldn't meet his eyes, so she looked behind the house to the slope. Brian raced around, eagerly showing his grandmother all his favorite climbing trees and hiding places in the woods. "Shouldn't have made love, or shouldn't have liked it?" Twyla asked.

"Both, I guess." He pushed away from the railing and started to pace. "I never meant to mislead you, Twyla, but I never told you the whole truth, either."

Oh, God, here it comes, she thought. He's married, or there was a bet riding on scoring with her, or— She shut off her thoughts. "What's the whole truth?"

"It's complicated."

"Lies are always complicated." She was so busy trying to understand what he was saying that she almost didn't hear the crunch of tires on gravel.

Shep did, barking madly at Reilly's old flatbed truck as it pulled to the side of the road. The passenger door opened.

Rob muttered something under his breath, something she didn't hear. His manner became that of a stranger as he walked toward the car. Twyla shooed the dog away and hurried after him, stunned to see a tall blond woman get out and wave to Reilly, thanking him for the ride. Then she turned to Rob and kissed him on the mouth.

For a long time.

Rob stepped back, a polite smile on his face. "Lauren," he said. "What are you doing here?"

"I got an earlier flight." The woman called Lauren wrinkled her dainty nose and took her hands away from him. "Heavens, what have you been doing? You're covered with horrid sweat."

Twyla didn't think his sweat was horrid. It was all she was capable of thinking as she walked down the drive toward them.

"How did you find me?" Rob asked.

"Were you hiding?" Lauren had a melodious voice and a classy accent, like a trained 1940s actress. She tilted her head back, laughing as she held out a hand to Twyla. "I'm Lauren DeVane."

Twyla took her slim, elegant hand. Killer manicure. "Hi. Twyla McCabe."

"Mr. Reilly was nice enough to give me a lift out here. Are you ready, darling?" Lauren asked Rob. Her smile was as dazzling as a toothpaste ad. "If we leave now, we can be in Chugwater in time for cocktail hour." She turned to Twyla. "We're meeting friends there," she explained.

Something about the statement made Twyla feel entirely excluded. She was pretty sure it was meant to sound that way.

"I'll get my keys." Rob spoke like a dead man. Or a doomed one, at least.

Which he was, Twyla thought, wondering if the steam coming out of her ears was visible. She heard nothing but guilt in the tone of his voice. So this was the "whole truth" he had been talking about earlier.

She found her voice somewhere in the shocked reaches of her throat. "Would you like a glass of lemonade, or maybe white wine?'' I have a nice jug of rat poison for Rob in the basement.

Lauren's faultlessly polite gaze flicked to the house, then to Rob. "You know, I truly would love to visit. I'm dying to hear all about your bachelor auction weekend. I want to know every single detail. A high school reunion is just too cute."

Rob stiffened with a sudden movement that seemed to jolt him out of his inertia. Twyla felt him looking at her, but she refused to meet his gaze, refused to diffuse the discomfort of the moment.

"I thought you were in a hurry to get to Chugwater," he said to Lauren.

"Yes, I suppose I was." She smiled apologetically at Twyla. "Maybe another time."

"Of course," Twyla replied, matching her lie for lie. She forced herself to address Rob. "I'll tell Brian and Mother you said goodbye."

He nodded. "Do that." He stuck out his hand and she took it, feeling the weight of Lauren's gaze on them and battling a swift, vivid memory of that warm, clever hand on her bare shoulder, then drifting down to her breast—

"Bye," she said, choking off the memory. "Thanks again…for fixing the porch."

She felt like a tree, rooted in place as they drove away. And she was proud of herself, really, because she forced herself to turn and walk with measured paces into the house, to climb the stairs and shut the door to her room before she broke down.

CHAPTER TWENTY

"DR. CARTER. Paging Dr. Carter."

Kneading away a crick in his neck, Rob saved a file on his laptop and went to answer the page. He had been working on a case involving a two-day-old term infant who had been rushed to the newborn intensive care unit in respiratory distress. The page was probably the coagulation studies he'd ordered.

As he took to the elevated walkway to the unit, the double doors at the end of the hall opened and a woman carrying an enormous bouquet of flowers came through. Colorful bursts of blossoms obscured her face, but he noticed immediately that she was wearing red shoes. A bright curl of red hair draped over her shoulder.

Before logic could take over, his heart leaped almost painfully in his chest and his mouth formed her name.

"Twyla?"

"Excuse me." Veering to one side, the woman with the flowers passed by, leaving a cloying hothouse fragrance behind.

He caught a glimpse of a pleasant face—not Twyla's.

"You're losing your mind, pal," he muttered under his breath, and continued down the hall to the nurses' station. He had to concentrate on the case, nothing but the case.

In the unit, he passed through a gauntlet of visitors, personnel in scrubs, drug sales reps. One of his techs waited at the desk, a sheaf of documents in hand and a look of triumph on his face.

"You were right," he said. "The coagulation results are consistent with your hunch. Too much heparin either in a line or the child."

"Thanks," said Rob, glad to have the problem isolated but not looking forward to sharing the results with the intensive care unit team. He grabbed the chart. "Did you page the baby's doctor?"

"He's with the team now. In C-Wing."

Tying on a surgical mask, Rob found the physicians and nurses clustered around a clear bassinet. The chart identified the child as "Baby Girl Gardner." Outside, the anxious parents paced, watching through the slatted blinds.

Rob and his team had worked overtime trying to figure out what the baby's symptoms added up to, and at last he'd figured it out. He regarded the small, struggling infant, trapped like a fly in a web of tubing and monitor wire.

The others stopped talking and waited expectantly.

"This infant," Rob said, "has been given an overdose of heparin."

"I beg your pardon," a nurse said, her voice hard with the iron of indignation. "This child has not been in the same room with a bottle of heparin."

Rob flipped to a page in his chart. "I figured someone would say that, so I ordered a heparin assay."

"Thank you, Doctor." A neonatologist Rob knew vaguely instantly ordered fresh frozen plasma. "We'll take it from here."

"Sorry," Rob said, trying to be polite. "That won't correct it. The infused plasma will only be contaminated with circulating heparin. That's your problem to begin with."

"So what do we do?"

"Protamine sulfate will reverse the overdose."

The neonatologist took the file from Rob. "Thanks a million. Good work."

"Just doing my job." Rob left the unit in a hurry, brushing past the nervous parents. His job was done. He'd just saved a baby's life. Yet part of him wanted to stay and see the little girl recover, blink her eyes and cry, respond to her mother's touch. That was what was missing from his practice, that vital connection.

It wasn't merely ego. He had asked himself that. He didn't crave the godlike adulation a primary-care physician got from his patients. It was the connection he wanted.

As he had so frequently over the long, hot summer, he pictured Twyla at the county hospital, combing out a patient's hair, those hands touching, stroking, healing as she listened.

Seeing her like that had made him question the choices he'd made. Knowing her, even for a brief time, had transformed him profoundly. She'd made him remember so many other facets of medicine. Yes, the pathology was vital, and his work in the field had been important. But in the process of being brilliant in the lab, was he losing his humanity?

Maybe it was time to try something else. Maybe the next step for him was to move out from behind the microscope. Sure, it got rough when you encountered a patient who didn't recover or wouldn't cooperate, but that came with the territory. He had been avoiding it for years.

Back in his suite in the hospital annex, he let the tech

know everything had worked out but declined the offer of going for a beer to celebrate. Closing the door to his office, he took off his lab coat, sat down at his desk and loosened his tie.

His paperweight was the horseshoe Twyla had given him. The one her father had declared a symbol of good luck. Rob didn't know why he kept it. The thing was a constant reminder of that weekend, and how Twyla had come to mean everything to him.

He picked up the horseshoe. "Okay, work, damn it. It's about time my luck came around."

The phone mocked him, a silent witness to his troubles over the summer. Prior to the bachelor auction, he'd thought his relationship with Lauren was fine—but knowing Twyla had made Rob aware of a gaping lack of true intimacy and understanding between him and Lauren.

After driving away from Twyla's house that day, he'd taken Lauren to see Lost Springs to show her where he came from.

"I don't want to get into the deep psychological implications of your returning here," she'd said, clearly uncomfortable as she'd fiddled with the latch of her designer purse. "You've triumphed over your circumstances. That's all that matters."

He used to believe that, but he knew better now. It wasn't all that mattered.

It had taken a hairdresser from Hell Creek, Wyoming, to make him realize that.

Lauren had cried when he'd told her it was over, but she hadn't tried to convince him to stay with her. She was no fool—she had probably seen the truth even before he had. She'd probably seen it the moment she'd walked up Twyla's drive that day.

Now September set the aspens aflame with bright golden color, and he still hadn't been in touch with Twyla. He'd tried calling, but she'd hung up. A hundred times more he had picked up that phone. But when he did, he wondered what he could possibly say to her that would convince her that, in one weekend, he had fallen completely in love with her, that knowing her had changed his life.

He knew damned well what she thought of him. Her face had said it all at their parting. He had betrayed her by not telling her about Lauren. Why should she trust him again?

A week after the reunion, a package had arrived. Rob's hopes had soared when he saw the postmark, then plummeted when he discovered the heavily insured contents: the ruby necklace he had given her, and the picture Gwen had taken of them before their weekend together. No note, no explanation. She really didn't need to explain. She had swept her life clean of him.

He knew he could go to her house, knock at her door, demand to be heard. But he wasn't ready to do that, not yet. He couldn't until he knew exactly what he had to offer her.

He turned the horseshoe over and over in his hands. He'd had all summer to think, to plan, to wonder, but when all was said and done, plans could take him only so far.

He glanced over at the fax machine to see that a message had come in while he was gone. Still holding the horseshoe, he looked at it—and his face broke into a huge smile. "Hot damn," he said. "It's about time."

Holding both his good-luck talisman and the letter, he experienced a strange lightness in his chest. Up until this moment, his life had been all about goal-setting and planning. Now he was about to take a blind plunge into a future he almost couldn't imagine. He was about to follow his instincts rather than his intellect. It was either the biggest mistake of his life…or the best move he could make.

CHAPTER TWENTY-ONE

THE BELL OVER THE SHOP door of Twyla's Tease 'n' Tweeze jangled as Gwen McCabe came in, bringing a fresh eddy of autumn air with her.

"Look what the wind blew in," Mrs. Duckworth declared, turning her head carefully under its covering of lavender-blue dye. "How's every little thing, hon?"

"Hectic," Gwen said, her color high from working outside. Ruefully she held her hands out to Diep. "Gardening hands. I'm a mess."

"You been working too hard," Diep said, leading her over to the manicure station. "All the time, work, work, work."

"I know," Gwen said, waving to Sadie and Mrs. Spinelli, who sat under the dryers, playing a game of gin. She sat down and swiveled around in an empty chair. "Isn't it glorious?"

Twyla felt a rush of gladness as she watched her mother. Gwen still got a little jumpy when she was away from the house, but she loved coming in to the salon to get "fixed up," as she put it.

She had been doing a lot of fixing up over the summer. She and Twyla had decided to give the farmhouse and yard a face-lift. Gwen had taken charge of the whole operation, supervising yard workers and painters and doing much of the work herself. Her eye for design and color had been invaluable in dreaming up color schemes for the paint job and garden layout. The house now wore a gleaming coat of white paint and sharp new louvered shutters in bright lemon yellow. Flower beds and shrubs bloomed in profusion, tended by Gwen.

Everything had improved over the summer—the house, the yard, Gwen, even Twyla's outlook on life. Everything except the emptiness carved out by memories of her brief lost weekend with Rob Carter.

She shouldn't have been surprised to discover that he was involved with Lauren DeVane, as beautiful and sophisticated as an ad in *Town & Country* magazine. Lauren was precisely the type of woman for him. She hobnobbed with the Fremonts and the Duncans. Twyla knew without asking that Lauren had been to finishing school, that she flew to New York City to shop, that she knew how to ski, and that she made regular trips to Europe. Twyla could even understand—or at least pretend to— why Rob hadn't told her about Lauren. The weekend in Hell Creek was a one-time event.

Still, the hurt had cut deep. He should have attended the reunion with her but left her heart alone. That was what an honorable man would have done. Instead, he'd taken all of her—body, heart, soul—and left nothing but emptiness. All along, he'd known he would go back to Lauren.

Even the well-meaning matchmakers had backed off from fixing Twyla up with more dates because she'd told them, "Don't do this to me anymore. I can't take it."

She pushed aside a feeling of melancholy and concentrated on Mrs. Duckworth's hair. Twyla wasn't the sort to drown in sorrow. It simply wasn't part of her makeup. With an almost defiant gratitude, her spirits lifted with each twist of the foil wrap. The women gossiped in low murmurs, and she thought how much she loved the sound of their voices and occasional laughter.

It was foolish to complain. Perhaps her life had not turned out as she'd thought it would, but like one of her mother's quilts, it was stitched together from bits and pieces, forming a whole that made her feel proud and fulfilled. She was a daughter, a mother, a business owner, and she liked the way things were.

Just as she was peeling off her gloves, a shadow fell over the front window of the shop. A gleaming black Lincoln Navigator parked in front. The back of it appeared to be crammed with boxes and luggage. Pressed against one window was a quilt.

Twyla did a double take. It was the quilt from the Lost Springs raffle.

"Would you look at that," Sadie Kittredge said, coming out from under her hair dryer. "Twyla, it's—"

"I know who it is." Her heart knocked almost painfully in her chest.

"Well, get out there and see what he wants, dear," Mrs. Spinelli said bossily. "Unless you want him to come in here."

"Let him come in here," Diep cried. "I want to have a word with this Dr. Hunk."

Twyla looked helplessly at her mother. Gwen inclined her head toward the door. "You'd better go out there," she said simply.

Twyla wiped her hands on her smock. She resisted the urge to glance in the mirror, but she couldn't keep from wishing she had time to freshen her makeup. She walked the walk of a condemned prisoner as she left the salon and stepped out on the sidewalk.

Rob got out of the truck. His hair was a little longer.

His smile still made her feel as if she were looking into the sun.

Please, she thought. Please, just let me get through this. Let me survive to the other side of the moment.

"I would have called first," he said, "but I haven't had much luck getting through to you."

He held out his hand to her, and like a fool, she took it.

Mistake. Alarm sirens shrieked through her. Let go, turn away, save yourself while you can.

"So how've you been?" he asked.

Outwardly nothing had changed. She still had the shop, still volunteered at the hospital. Brian was in second grade now. Her mother went to the grocery store once a week, to Quilt Quorum, to church. She had worked all summer on the house, and it had never looked better. No dramatic changes, but everything had started on that strangest of days, the day of the bachelor auction.

"I've been fine," she said.

"Let's walk," he suggested.

"No, thanks." She extracted her hand from his.

"Fine, we'll talk here. It'll give the ladies in your shop and the customers at the Grill something to gossip about."

She opened her mouth to protest but decided against it. He was right, damn him. The idea of making a scene in the middle of town made her feel faint. Still refusing to see or speak to him was childish. Cowardly. She had conquered her fears by going to her reunion. Learned to face the things that hurt her—like Dr. Robert Carter.

"All right," she said levelly, "why are you here?"

He didn't waste any time. He took out a black velvet box with a familiar logo.

"Oh, no," she said. "I sent the necklace back to you because I never want to see it again."

"I traded it in for this." He snapped open the box.

Before she could stop herself, she gasped with unguarded surprise. From the corner of her eye, she saw someone come out of the feed store, and a car drove past. Suddenly she wished she'd taken him up on his offer to go somewhere private.

Scrambling to gather her wits, she tried to pretend she wasn't interested. But no amount of pretense could mask her amazement at the beautiful oval-cut ruby ring encrusted with diamonds.

He took her hand and slid it on her ring finger, and like an idiot, she let him.

He kept hold of her hand and said, "I want to marry you, Twyla."

First longing—just a painful flash—seized her. Then a car horn sounded somewhere, and reality set in. She forced out a burst of laughter and snatched her hand away. "Okay, very funny. How much did Mrs. Spinelli pay you to say that?"

"I mean it, Twyla." Those eyes. Deep velvet brown, and so sincere she wanted to smack him.

"Our relationship—if you can even call it that—started out a lie. How can you want to marry me?"

"Twyla, knowing you for just one weekend changed my life. I want to be with you and Brian. I want to give you everything. Your degree in psychology. A trip to France. Your dream house, anything—"

She laughed again, but heard bitterness beneath the laughter. "You're too late," she said, trying not to love the rich weight of the ring on her finger. "Everything changed for me that weekend, too. I discovered I'm perfectly happy here, doing what I do. It's probably hard for a busy city doctor to understand, but there you are. My place is here, in this small town, doing people's hair and listening to their troubles.''

She could feel the tears pressing and burning at the backs of her eyes. She prayed she wouldn't shed them. "I don't need to get a degree to turn me into a good friend and a good listener. I already know how to be those things. I don't need to go to Paris in order to be more sophisticated, because I found out I don't much care for sophistication.''

"But, Twyla—''

"No, let me finish.'' She had to get it all out before she broke down. "I agonized, wondering if you would have come to me on bended knee if I had a degree, if I'd been to Paris, if I'd been somebody important. And then I decided I am somebody important, just not to you.''

He stuck his thumb into his belt and stood straighter, his posture mildly daunting. "Who the hell told you what I think, what I feel?''

The postman walked by, slowing his pace as he passed them. Twyla figured he was straining to hear the conversation. Then a waitress came out of the Grill, choosing that precise moment to sweep the sidewalk, stirring the smell of dry autumn leaves with a wide push broom.

Flushing with embarrassment, Twyla dropped her voice. "Intuition. I don't need a degree to tell me that.''

"Then your intuition is way off.'' He ran his finger down her arm, and she braced herself, hoping his touch wouldn't make her shiver. But it did, just as it had the first time he'd touched her.

"Couldn't you feel it happening that weekend?'' he asked. "The last thing I expected was to meet someone like you. Someone I can trust…tell about Lost Springs. Someone who can show me the things that are real. The last thing I expected was to fall in love with you.''

She bit the inside of her cheek, staving off sobs of surprise and yearning. Oh Lord, she thought, don't do this. Don't let me want this to be real.

''I'm not good at long-distance relationships,'' she stated. ''And I really don't want to live in Denver.''

''Fine,'' he said. ''Because I don't live in Denver anymore.''

''You don't?''

''Nope. Sold my condo and my interest in the practice. I'm looking for a new place.''

''Why did you do that?''

''It would be too long a commute to Converse County Hospital.'' He handed her a wrinkled fax with an official-looking letterhead. ''It took me all summer to get everything arranged. My license to practice in Wyoming is being approved.''

''*My* Converse County Hospital?''

''Yep. I'm getting out of lab work. I'll be on staff beginning next month.'' He stroked her arm again, lightly coaxing. ''So what do you say? Can we start over? Swear to God I'll get it right this time.''

''Give me a minute.'' Shaking, terrified, she went into the shop, pressing herself against the wall and closing her eyes while the tears squeezed out from under her lids.

''Twyla, honey, what's wrong?'' asked her mother.

Everyone gathered around. Diep grabbed her hand. ''A ring! He gave you a ring!'' They oohed and aahed over it while Twyla tried to collect herself.

''He says he fell in love with me,'' she confessed.

Her mother began to cry, too, hugging Twyla. "Oh, sweetie. I knew it. I just knew it."

"He wants to marry me." Twyla could barely say it aloud.

Sadie rolled her eyes dramatically. "Oh, there's a disaster."

"A fate worse than death," Mrs. Duckworth added, handing her a tissue.

"And to think she could have had that bald mortician bachelor from Terre Haute," Mrs. Spinelli pointed out.

"Yeah, any woman in her right mind would take him over George Clooney," Sadie said.

"Aw, come on, Twyla," Diep said. "If you say yes to Rob, you get to keep the ring."

"Do you know how much I'd like to have that man for a son-in-law?" Gwen added.

"Well." She snuffled into the tissue. "Since you put it that way..."

She put her hand on the doorknob and turned to her mother one last time. "Okay, Mom, this is it. You can still try to talk me out of it."

Gwen shook her head, a telltale gleam of happiness in her eye. She patted Twyla's cheeks, drying the tears. "Fat chance, dear. Fat chance indeed."

Twyla stepped cautiously onto the sidewalk again. Rob leaned against his truck, ankles crossed, looking nonchalant—except that his temples glistened with sweat.

"Sorry," Twyla said, a crazy smile trying to break free. "You just sprang this on me so suddenly."

"And you had to consult with the committee."

She gave a watery laugh and resisted the impulse to pinch herself. "My mom, mainly."

"It's nice, having a mom. So what'd she say?"

"That she'd love to have you for a son-in-law."

"What about you, Twyla?"

"I love you, period. I do, Rob. I love you so much I can't think."

"Good. Get in the car."

"What? But I—" She glanced uncertainly at the shop. In unison, the ladies inside made vigorous shooing motions with their hands. Embracing the insanity of the moment, she climbed in, and he drove down the dirt road he'd shown her after giving her the tour of Lost Springs.

Giddiness rose in her. "I remember this place. This is Lovers' Lane."

He grinned, parking in a shaded spot on the bluff overlooking Lightning Creek. He turned off the car but left the radio playing softly. He slid his arm across the back of the seat and put his mouth so close to hers she could almost taste him. "Then you know," he said, "why I brought you here."

He spread the raffle quilt on the ground. She took off her shoes and ran her bare foot over the soft, worn surface. "You must have thought I was so gauche the day you bought all those tickets from me," she said.

"I remember thinking a lot of things about you when we first met." He put his arm around her waist and brought her swiftly against him. "But 'gauche' wasn't one of them. Earnest, maybe. Also funny and sexy and smart."

"Really?"

"Really." With slow deliberation he undid the buttons of her uniform, one by one. "Do you think I could've made myself go to your ten-year reunion if I'd thought anything less of you?"

Her skin heated where his fingers brushed over it. "That was definitely beyond the call of duty. I thought you were so polished and sophisticated. I was sure you were laughing at me behind my back the whole time."

"I was putty in your hands from the first moment I saw you, Twyla," he whispered, his breath warm in her ear. "Putty in your hands." His slow deliberation shifted into high gear, and suddenly Twyla couldn't wait to be out of her clothes, to be with him. After all the weeks of thinking she'd never see him again, never be like this again, she needed to be close to him, next to him…now.

They made love like a couple of teenagers, with that level of arousal and urgency and probably, she thought without regret, that same lack of grace and finesse, barely even removing their clothes in their eagerness. Except that when Twyla was a teenager, it had been nothing like this afterward. Instead of a guilty, embarrassed ride home, they lazed, half-clothed and fully sated, in the autumn sun. The hollow of his shoulder cradled her head so perfectly she never wanted to move.

He picked up one of the red clogs she wore to work. "When I caught myself fantasizing about red shoes all summer," he confessed, "I knew it had to be love."

She laughed and shifted position so she could look at him—open shirt, jeans unbuttoned and half-unzipped. And that face. How could she have survived a whole summer without seeing that face? But her common-sense fairy came knocking, and she felt compelled to say, "This is all happening so fast, Rob. Maybe we should make sure it isn't just hormones, that it's the real thing."

"Do we really care?" he asked.

"The grown-up answer would be to say yes. We should give this some time, see if it could really work," she said.

"Fine, then you say yes."

"Yes." She frowned, feeling light-headed with wonder and awakening joy. Her fingers shook a little as she refastened the buttons of her uniform. Somehow, the situation seemed to demand a little dignity. "But I, um, forgot the question."

"The question was 'Will you marry me?'"

"And I just said yes?"

He nodded. "You're totally committed."

Something didn't add up, but as she stared into his eyes, she felt herself teetering, wavering on the edge. Then she let herself plunge into something that felt so right. "I am," she said.

He shut his eyes, and for a moment he looked totally vulnerable. Then he faced her and said, "Do you know, I never wanted anything as much as I wanted you? To be with you, live with you, to be Brian's dad? I had no idea what it was like to want someone until I met you."

Her heart full, she lifted her head to kiss him, and they were lost again, lost in each other and in the wonder of the step they were about to take.

A while—quite a long while—later, he propped himself up on one elbow and said, "You know we can't begin our life together with a lie."

Oh, God, she thought. Here it comes. Something about the girlfriend—

He laughed at her expression and dug in his jeans pocket. "I didn't really trade in the necklace for the ring." He held the necklace aloft, diamond and ruby facets catching the sunlight. He sat her up and clasped it around her neck, pausing now and then to kiss and nip the back of her neck.

"I couldn't stand the idea of taking it back." His lips traced the pulse at the side of her throat. "Because I kept remembering—this necklace was the only thing you had on the first time I made love to you."

She shut her eyes. "I remember that, too."

"Then I hope like hell you remember how sexy it was."

She was so replete with happiness that she felt compelled to say, "I have a confession of my own to make. About that offer to take me to Paris?"

"Ah. The place you said you don't need to see because you're already fulfilled."

"Maybe I was a bit hasty there. Saying I didn't need to go. That was just a manner of speaking—to prove my point that I can be happy with my life even though I'll never have Paris."

"So what are you saying?"

"Just that…if you really insist on it, I'd be glad to visit Paris with you."

"I hear it's a great place for a honeymoon. But I don't know…"

"What?"

"You might become too sophisticated for me, and there'd be no living with you."

She turned, unbuttoning the front of her uniform and parting it to display the glittering necklace. "That's a risk you'll have to take, Dr. Carter."

His eyelids closed halfway. "Okay, Paris it is. But promise me something."

"Anything," she said.

"Wear those red shoes for the wedding. And never, ever cut your hair."

"I'll do the red shoes thing, even though people will talk. The hair…we'll see."

HEART OF THE WEST

continues with

COURTING CALLIE

by

Lynn Erickson

Widower Mase LeBow figures that Callie Thorne's
remote ranch is the best place to keep his son out of
harm's way. So he's determined to charm her after she
"buys" him for a date. But her insistence on helping his
troubled boy irks him, her flights of fancy amuse him,
and her off-beat manner gets under his skin. Falling in
love with Callie when his life is being threatened has got
to be a huge mistake!

Available in August

Here's a preview!

"CLOSE THE DOOR gently if you can, so you don't startle her."

Zeke glanced at Katherine and caught his breath. Her green blouse was unfastened, although she'd modestly pulled it around her so that her breast barely showed. Somehow that made the picture more erotic to Zeke. Rain drummed on the roof of the truck but he could still hear the soft sucking noises Amanda made while she nursed.

He pulled the door closed as best he could, knowing he'd have to open it and slam it again before they started driving. Then he stared straight ahead and tried to concentrate on following the path of an individual raindrop as it slid down the windshield. He seemed to be having trouble getting enough air, and he cracked his window open a little.

A woman nursing her child was no big deal, he told himself. He lived among wild animals who raised their young that way, and this was the same thing. Except it wasn't even close. A year ago, he'd desperately wanted this woman, and she'd desperately wanted him. Now, the result of their mating that night lay in her arms, the tiny mouth fastened to her breast. God help him, he wanted this woman still.

"There's no way to fix the tire, is there?" Katherine asked quietly.

"No." He cleared the hoarseness from his throat, hoping she didn't notice. He didn't want her to know how she still affected him.

"Maybe someone will come along."

"That's not likely." He took a deep breath and let it out. "We're going to have to drive with the tire flat. I have a cabin out here. It's not far. From there we can call a tow truck."

"You live out here?"

"Yeah, when I'm not on duty at the park. It beats renting an apartment somewhere."

She nodded. "I can't picture you in an apartment. I imagine you clearing the land and building something out of logs, like Daniel Boone or Davy Crockett."

Zeke grinned. "Which is exactly what I did."

Katherine gazed at him, her expression wistful. "That's the first time you've smiled since we met at the lodge."

"Yeah, well, this experience hasn't been a laugh a minute," Zeke said wryly.

"But Amanda is such a beautiful little girl. I wish you could share some of the joy I feel."

"You're really happy about this?" he asked.

"How could I help being happy? Maybe I was a bit shocked when the doctor told me I was pregnant, but in about five minutes the shock wore off and I started feeling excited. A new life was growing inside me. That's a miraculous thing, Zeke."

He wondered if he'd have reacted that positively if she'd called to tell him right away. Maybe not, but he'd never know. Well-meaning though she might have been, she'd cheated him out of that sense of anticipation.

Katherine made a slight turn toward him, tempting him again with the perfect picture of motherhood that she represented. "My only regret is whatever trouble I'm causing you."

Zeke looked away, breaking eye contact. "You haven't caused me any trouble," he said. *"Yet."*

Harlequin Romance®

Delightful

Affectionate

Romantic

Emotional

Tender

Original

Daring

Riveting

Enchanting

Adventurous

Moving

Harlequin Romance—the
series that has it all!

HROM-G

HARLEQUIN PRESENTS®

HARLEQUIN PRESENTS
men you won't be able to resist
falling in love with...

HARLEQUIN PRESENTS
women who have feelings
just like your own...

HARLEQUIN PRESENTS
powerful passion in
exotic international settings...

HARLEQUIN PRESENTS
intense, dramatic stories that will keep you
turning to the very last page...

HARLEQUIN PRESENTS
The world's bestselling romance series!

Harlequin® Historical

From rugged lawmen and
valiant knights to defiant heiresses
and spirited frontierswomen,
Harlequin Historicals will
capture your imagination with
their dramatic scope, passion
and adventure.

Harlequin Historicals...
they're too good to miss!

HARLEQUIN®

A M E R I C A N ◆ R O M A N C E®

LOOK FOR OUR FOUR FABULOUS MEN!

Each month some of today's bestselling authors bring
four new fabulous men to Harlequin American Romance.
Whether they're rebel ranchers, millionaire power brokers
or sexy single dads, they're all gallant princes—and
they're all ready to sweep you into lighthearted fantasies
and contemporary fairy tales where anything is possible
and where all your dreams come true!

You don't even have to make a wish…
Harlequin American Romance will grant your every desire!

Look for Harlequin American Romance
wherever Harlequin books are sold!